DEBUSSY'S SLIPPERS

To Louise

I hope you enjoy
George Gershwin's
adventures as much
as Severus!
All the best
Steve

Steve Exeter

Copyright © 2020 Steve Exeter

All rights reserved.

First Edition

ISBN: 9798710506202

For my wife, Jennie and son, Horatio
with love and gratitude

"Life is a lot like jazz… it's best when you improvise."

– George Gershwin

CHAPTER 1

George Gershwin's body lies cold on a surgical table. The operating room around him is draped in a black and white haze. The team of surgeons and nurses remain unseen. Only their muffled voices can be heard. Miniature showgirls appear in Gershwin's ear canal, dancing in synchronised choreography along the relatively giant ridges. They dance toward the light of the operating room, out of the darkness of George's inner ear. Gershwin's once-powerful mind is fading, the shadows groping like fingers of slow and gradual death, into the harsh fluorescent light of the sterilised theatre.

Further into the murky ear canals, giant cogs and hexagonal cells are being taken down and packed away. Boiler-suited workmen wipe their brows in unison, then flick on their headlamps to finish the job. They step and jive as if dancing, working to dismantle Gershwin's brain. Like the showgirls, they seem to be guided by inner music.

Water gushes in, flooding the inside of the other-worldly arena. The showgirls surf down the spilling waves and dissolve into the harsh light, while the boiler-suited workmen vaporise and reform underwater. They've shifted to the form of synchronised swimmers in swan costumes, dancing a streamlined ballet in the gentle current.

A great wave rolls down the ear canal, losing the gears, cogs and wheels of his genius brain, sending the dancing swimmers down to the drain in the tile floor. The swimmers succumb to the typhoon and the drain, while the pieces of George's brain swirl around, and the dream-fog of transfigured memory begins to clear. When the black and white haze lifts, the team of surgeons can be seen hovering over the body and flitting about the room. The flustered medical staff try to administer a last-ditch effort to save Gershwin.

Dr Dandy, an elegant man in his early 40s, scoffs loudly at the incompetence of the lead surgeons and candy-stripers. "Catawampus... what a mess," he mutters to himself.

The lead surgeon, Dr Carlton Phipps, steps back from the surgical table in a droll stupor. He seems to have forgotten just what he had meant to do. He cocks his head to Dandy with a vacant expression. "Should we proceed with the anaesthetic?"

Dr Dandy leers at him, then calls back over his shoulder as he begins to scrub in. "He hasn't even been prepared for surgery?"

"Why, no," Dr Phipps says. "We were instructed to wait for you, and I thought it unwise to act rashly, given the sensitivity. Such a high-profile patient..."

Dr Dandy dries his hands in a livid rage. "What sort of blunt force trauma have you sustained, man? These young doctors are all bedside manner and no balls. You have a dying patient on your hands, and you're worried about what the press will say? What sort of operation is this? Who told you to wait?"

Dr Phipps pauses a moment, unperturbed, but still numb and confused. "The medical director, Sir. He said you were coming post-haste, and we were trying to be careful is all; ducks in a row..." He shakes his head. Saying something so childish snaps him out of his daze. "Besides, the man's a celebrity."

Dr Dandy throws up his hands. "Celebrity… Whatever! You've got Broadway up the street! You should be used to celebrities!"

Dr Phipps at last takes action. "General anaesthetic," he tells the lead nurse. "Stat."

She nods to an orderly, who prepares the anaesthetic. Then she points to Gershwin's eyelids. "Doctor, you should see this. There's some eye movement."

Dandy frowns at Phipps, wondering why the nurse is taking more charge than Phipps is, and goes to pull up Gershwin's eyelid. Taking note of the faint vitality in the eyes, he leans into George's ear, using it like a candlestick phone receiver. "Mr Gershwin?" he shouts, "are you there?"

Gershwin murmurs back. Dandy puts his ears to George's lips, but the whispers are too soft to make out. George sinks back with his eyes closed.

"I've lost his pulse," another nurse says.

The surgeon looks over at Dr Dandy. "Well, now that you're here… what do you advise?"

"He's dead, you imbeciles…" Dandy glares

at everyone in the room, but sends an especially piercing gaze to Dr Phipps. He turns on his heel and stomps into the hallway, where he's met by a military escort.

"Well," Dr Dandy nods to his escort with a solemn expression. "We lost him. For our sake, I'm happy it wasn't the commander in chief after all. I was far too late to be of any service. The hospital staff here is incorrigible... A tragedy."

"I'm sorry, Sir," the escorting officer says, "and for the record, everything that happened here today is strictly classified."

"Yes," Dr Dandy replies. "Oh, yes. Believe me... I won't divulge one moment of this debacle. Now, if it's not too much trouble, I'll just write up the necessary paperwork, and then perhaps the US Navy would find me a hotel? I can't manage a trip back to the harbour tonight."

"Don't worry, Sir," another officer chimes in. "That's already been taken care of."

Dr Dandy nods curtly. The escort leads him past the family waiting room, where a man and a woman are bickering. Ira Gershwin, George's forty-year-old brother, sits between them.

Ira Gershwin is flumped into a contour seat, looking despondent as the other two volley retorts. Ira is unshaven, haggard, and weary. He covers his ears with his head in his hands. His two companions are Wally Roberts and Kitty Carlisle. By now their disagreement is such that they are nearly at each other's throats. As Ira tries to tune them out, he wonders why they don't seem to mind causing a scene in a hospital waiting room.

At last Ira steps in to break them up, but the impulse is too aggressive and tactless to have a mollifying effect. "Watch what you're saying," he says pointing his finger at Kitty.

"Ahh, blow it out your ass, Ira!" Kitty says before he even finishes, flipping her blond hair over her shoulder.

"Both of you shut up," Wally says in his know-it-all-manner. "George might not get outa this."

Ira stands up and gets into Wally's face. There was a limit he would allow with Wally – but this was too far. "Don't say that, don't even *think* it."

But Kitty agrees, "It's true and you know it, Ira. Don't pretend like you really care when it's guilt you're feeling. You know he never wanted to go to

Hollywood. You're the one who took him there." Her eyes were cold with resentment.

Ira turned to Kitty, who was only a few inches shorter, and tried to scoff with conviction. He spoke to her as if she weren't in the room, although he was glaring right at her. "Is she starting in on Hollywood again? It was good for me, and it was even better for George!"

Tears pool in Kitty's long lashes, refusing to fall as her lips quiver. "Good for your bank balance," she sobs, then turns away to weep in one of the plastic chairs. In the calm and quiet of the late-night waiting room, her tinny cries echo off the plasterboard walls.

Ira's teeth were on edge. "How would you know anyway?" he shouts down at her shivering shoulders. "Were you there? We had some good times. Maybe that's what's getting to you, Kitty. Maybe you're the one who's guilty, because you couldn't keep him in New York. Well it's not about you. There was a lot he didn't like about New York, too."

Wally takes pity on Kitty, who's weeping more heavily at the harsh words from Ira. he sits down beside her to rub her back, then looks to Ira. "Come now, man, lay off it. You'd like to see a woman cry harder to buoy up your own benefit?"

Ira continues, ignoring Wally's reproach. "Face it Kitty, you couldn't keep him. Hollywood was the right next step for both of us, and you had your chance to move out there. But you balked. Typical if you ask me."

Wally sighs, ready to make peace as the voice of reason. "If we don't cut this out, we're all going to say things we'll regret. It was nobody's fault that George got so caught up. It was just the lifestyle… Nobody's to blame. And it might've happened in this city, too."

Kitty wants the last word, and looks up at Ira. "You never read the letters he wrote to me. We could've been happy here. He loved me and you pulled him away with your money-grabbing pressure. You should have known better than to put your own brother on this path. And look where we ended up. It's no wonder he wanted to be flown back here for his treatment."

Ira looks into Kitty's red-rimmed eyes and finally takes pity. He blinks at her, sighs and sinks back into his chair. Kitty weeps quietly as Wally hushes her, telling her everything will be fine, that George will pull through. Ira puts his face in his hands and rubs his eyes. He can still hope for the best. That's all that he has left.

***

When Dr Dandy arrives at his downtown hotel, he leaves his bag with the bellboy and goes straight to the hotel bar, where he orders a scotch. An African-American pianist plays 'Love is Here to Stay'. He finishes the piece with a flourish then announces a five-minute break between songs. A waiter comes over to refill his brandy glass.

Dr Dandy saunters over to the piano. "That's a Gershwin tune, isn't it?"

"Yes sir," the pianist says, sipping his brandy, "what a tragedy. I just heard of his passing as I put the set together, so I added this number in his honour."

"I understand that he wrote wonderful music, but why was he so popular?" Dr Dandy asks. "After all, it's 1937. There's no shortage of that sort of musician in these parts."

"Oh, but he was a very fine musician. He could really write a melody. Things that were at once simple, stripped down, and yet bent the ear. You couldn't help but tap your feet. He had a great sense of rhythm for a white man."

As Dandy learns a little more about George through the lens of a fellow musician, Ira Gershwin walks into the hotel lobby and spies Dr Dandy. Looking drawn and tired, Ira comes up to the piano, just as the pianist is finishing his break and turning back to the keys.

"Excuse me, Dr Dandy? I'm Ira Gershwin, George's brother. I apologise for not getting a chance to talk to you earlier. You, uh… I'd like to thank you… I've got a cab outside. Do you have a moment to take a ride with me?"

Dr Dandy considers Ira for a moment, and with a mix of genuine interest and pity, decides to follow along. After all, he's been plucked from his typical routine and feels justified with another twist to what's developing into a more and more alternative evening. Ira shakes his hand graciously and leads the doctor to the taxi idling out front.

"Broadway," Ira says, as the cab crawls down the famous avenue. "This is where George I had our first big break," he sighed. "Looking back now, they were some of our happiest times."

Dr Dandy turns to Ira with curiosity. "So, you're not from Hollywood originally?"

"Hell no," Ira chuckles. "We only moved out there last year. Our family is still here. New York born and bred."

"As I understand it," Dandy says, "George was quite the travelling man."

Ira chuckles again, but another wave of sorrow rolls in, and he clears his throat, suddenly very dry. "He considered himself a worldly gentleman."

Dr Dandy nods. "From the big city to Tinseltown," Dandy says, "and over the big blue to Europe, right?"

"That's so," Ira nods.

"And what did he achieve by going to Paris?" Dandy asks.

"Search me," Ira says, a little mournfully. "He said he was dissatisfied. Needed more inspiration. Needed to be in touch with another *level* of art. 'Capital-A' *Art*, I suppose. He thought he hadn't really made it yet."

"And he thought he needed to raise the stakes somehow?"

Ira mulls over this perspective. "You could say that, I suppose. He understood the recognition he received on Broadway, but it had more to do with the sort of respect he wanted."

"He wanted the respect of the world?" Dandy asks.

"I think that's it. Perhaps the theatre scene was sort of a small pond for him. He thought if he crossed the ocean, he could swim with the legends of music… all the great composers. I really admired him for that, but I didn't see the rush he was in. Sometimes I think his sights were set too high, always with a vision for what a venture would *lead* to, that he lost the pleasure of the composition at hand. I was always happy to be the toast of Broadway."

Dandy smiles. "It does have a certain appeal."

Ira returns the smile, trying his best to be modest. "I used to think I was just the man who put words to George's music. But when Lorenz Hart called me The Jeweller, I realised I had a reputation in my own right. I wasn't ever as famous as George was, but there was enough champagne and caviar to go around. I guess I was just a little more content than George. Even as kids, he was always pushing the envelope, trying to be the best."

"Well," Dandy says with a sympathetic shift in tone, "working with your family can often be complicated. But it seems both of you got along well together."

"When all's said and done," Ira nods, "I have to say I agree."

With that, the two men sit in silence as the taxi heads for the Gershwin family home. Upon arrival, Ira's wife appears in the foyer, while Ira has offered to give Dandy a quick tour, the doctor waves him off modestly. Ira nods with understanding then goes up to kiss Leonore. "Dr Dandy, this is my wife, Leonore."

Leonore smiles. "Good evening, Doctor. It's a pleasure to meet you." She turns back to her husband. "Honey, you had a call from California. I took down a message and left it by the phone."

"I'd better deal with that now," Ira says, already hurrying to the phone as he calls over his shoulder towards Leonore, "Would you mind fixing the doctor a drink?"

When Ira goes into his study and shuts the door, his hand wavers a moment over the note which Leonore took down. Before he picks it up, he takes the moment to lean back against the wall and quietly weep for a few moments. The message is of course to do with business – a project which George had been involved in along with him, and the flash-memory of the past few tragic days washes over him. As he wipes his tears and tries to collect himself, he can hear murmuring from Dandy and Leonore in the other room.

Leonore shows Dandy a seat in the family room. Although it's well furnished, there's something oddly un-lived-in about the warmly-lit home. Dr Dandy scans the room with a perfunctory glance, careful not to linger upon anything for long, which might suggest judgement of the decor. But he can't help but notice a magnitude of photographs of the two brothers, and almost a full wall of mementos; trophies, plaques and record albums, a toast to their achievements.

Leonore folds her hands behind her back.

"About that drink. What'll it be, Doc?"

"Scotch, please," Dandy says. "If that's not too much trouble. I know it's late."

"On the rocks or neat?" she asks politely.

"Rocks, thank you," he says.

"No trouble at all." She goes to the bar caddy and begins fixing his drink. "Ira's found this hard to accept. I've been concerned with how he would react when the inevitable happened."

"Inevitable?" Dandy asks, increasingly captivated by the nuances of the late composer's life. A man who he is finding it more and more painful that he couldn't save. But Dandy was the sort of fellow to confront his inauspicious feelings, to travel the dark paths of intrigue that got to the root of things. Dandy, at times, felt he subsisted on depth, and that anything shallow hardly served him.

"If you knew George," she says, "you'd have come to the same conclusion. The way he lived, I really don't believe that he ever thought about the long term. He never stopped."

"And Ira always worked with him?" Dandy asks. "Professionally, I mean?"

She hands him a glass of single malt and sighs. "Ira took responsibility for George in a way and that was a tremendous strain on him." Leonore looks back at the door to the study, to account for the possibility that Ira's ears were burning. "Between you and me, I think Ira and I were the only stability George ever had."

Dandy swirls his scotch, the ice cubes twinkling. "He never married?"

Leonore laughs, "God no, not George. He wasn't what you'd describe as the marrying kind. There were a few that got close to him. Kitty for one... she was at the hospital earlier tonight. With Ira, I believe. Anyway, she doted on George for years, and by the way she was the kind of woman any man would be happy to marry. But even Kitty couldn't tie old George Gershwin down. But they met a long time ago, when George and Ira were just starting on Broadway, around the early twenties..."

CHAPTER 2

In a dimly-lit 1920s nightclub in Manhattan, a group of comically corpulent and gregarious financiers, chortle and clink glasses to celebrate George and Ira's latest Broadway hit.

"To the most dashing hands to ever tickle the ivories!" one of the men gloats, raising his glass as high as his stubby arm will lift it.

George and Ira are nestled in the middle of two of them, holding onto their own glasses with their elbows tucked in.

"Leaving *our* hands to count the monies," another financier declares with pride.

Ira laughs, jabbing George in the ribs to get him to play along. "Oh, boys. You're an incredible lot—"

"Pish-posh," an especially loud gentleman cuts in. "So long as you and he write the songs, we'll write the cheques!"

The men let out belly laughs and cheer together

again, spilling champagne over their greasy, sausage-hands.

Ira grins. "Well said, and for that, we thank you!" He turns to George as the other men take big drinks from their glasses. Ira hopes George will add something here, to butter up the gang of portly playboys. But a quiet moment passes, and George doesn't say a word.

"Say something," Ira murmurs to George under his breath.

George, at last taking the hint, clears his throat and says, "Indeed!"

The men laugh, wallop and cheer again while George takes the chance to slide out from the booth. Ira shakes hands on his behalf, grinning broadly, then scurries after George.

When he catches up, George mutters to Ira softly, "These men are incorrigible."

Ira just rolls his eyes and tries to let it go. After all, by now they're out of earshot, and although he wouldn't say it to their faces, Ira agrees.

George approaches the bar and takes an unlit cigarette right out of a white-gloved hand. An attractive young woman turns and throws daggers with her eyes.

"Dearest Miss, do you mind?" George says as he pretends to puff on the cigarette, making the motion of striking up a lighter.

The young woman's suitor leans in and says sarcastically, "She does mind." But he lights up the cigarette for George anyhow.

Ira steps in between, before it gets any worse. "Sir, my apologies. Ira Gershwin…" He offers the suitor his hand, who shakes it demurely. "And this is my brother, George. He's just blowing off steam, quite like a chimney—"

"Gershwin," the suitor interjects with interest. "The piano fellow?"

A moment passes and George turns to Ira this time, for now that his quarry is guarded, he has no time for this conversation. He whispers, "Say something," to Ira, then turns to scan the room for available young ladies.

Ira gives George a frosty eye then returns his gaze to the suitor. "Indeed. I write the lyrics, he writes the bars. Have you seen the latest?"

But the suitor and his companion seem to have lost interest, and turn their attention to the conversation further down the bar. George finds solace in his hijacked cigarette. They mosey on over and stake their own territory at the far end of the bar.

"Brash bunch," Ira says, nodding back at the couple.

George gives him an impish look. "You drove them away, I think."

Ira sighs, hardly knowing how to take his brother seriously. "You know, George, you have to schmooze a bit with the men who are paying us."

"Eh," George shrugs. "They'll inebriate, then copulate with random frolicking legs, and they won't remember anything else... Which is the very reason why they'll write us another cheque."

Ira smiles despite himself. "You're so bitter, brother."

"It's Broadway. It's Hollywood with a bit more nerves. I'd be more inclined to converse if the quality of these formulaic showtunes warranted it." George takes a long drag on his cigarette and without missing a beat says, "Who's that?"

Ira looks around. "Who?"

George nods discreetly. "The life of the room

over there."

A young woman twirls her cigarette holder like a weapon; she's the spitting image of young Katharine Hepburn, surrounded by a wealth of suitors.

"*You're* the light of the room," Ira says. "If you'd just flicker a bit."

George ignores the compliment. "Are they guests from the show?"

"How should I know? I can barely see who it is from here!"

But George is already walking off, having missed Ira's comment.

"Glad you asked," Ira mutters.

George strolls right up to the group, but the ring of gentleman callers is a few rows deep, so he hangs around the edges like a lightning bug looking to get lucky.

The light of the room gives an ironic laugh. "A bit glib, don't you think?"

George watches a suitor step back as if stabbed in the chest by her rejection. George wrestles around the perimeter, trying for a better look at the apple of these men's eyes. All the while, more of the men try to curry her favour.

"The theatre is merely painted gold, my dear," one suitor says. "An echo chamber for pauper patrons to polish their cheeks with tears otherwise reserved for fears of poverty. Soon they'll all be behind tubes watching whatever farces gas out some Californian's derrière."

George turns sour as he hears this. He knows he can do better than to take cheap shots at Hollywood's link to the American upper class.

"If they had any courage, they'd at least channel a morsel of a talent like Mozart," another suitor jokes.

The group laughs and George bites his lip, still vying for a way in.

When the laughter fades, the young woman speaks up. "Now, if an opera's beauty had the wit of Broadway; that would be a show!"

The group laughs even more heartily.

"Wit of Broadway," George whispers to himself, as if to savour the velvet sound of her voice. He turns tail and rushes to the piano across from the bar and sits down. Within seconds, he begins to play. He's channelling pieces of 'By Strauss', putting the melody against a more standard, classical approach.

Ira comes over looking curious, his eyebrows perched high upon his forehead "An encore?"

"Just a ditty…" George replies, playing by memory and looking up, trying to see if the mysterious woman has noticed him playing.

Meanwhile, the financiers clash their cutlery together and bellow with cheers and laughter, as if in honour of some medieval royal tradition. George sneers at them a moment then turns his eyes back to the young Katharine Hepburn lookalike.

"Is this a future work?" Ira asks, leaning on the piano. "Perhaps I should tell those gents to stay keen."

George scoffs and continues to dance his hands across the keys. He couldn't care less about the men at the table, and he's annoyed that Ira can't see this. "Ira, I'm just having a little fun, can you let me focus?"

Just as he darts his eyes back to the young woman and the gaggle of suitors, she turns to the piano and locks eyes with George. Like an involuntary kick-back, George slides into a sweeping flourish of tones. The gentlemen clamour and shout their approval, drowning out the very music with which George hopes to reach his heart's desire. But the glint in her eyes fades and she turns back to the group of grovelling men.

"Wonderful," George mutters, a little disappointed. "Those deep-pocketed brutes got in the way again."

Ira seems to understand and puts a hand on his brother's shoulder. "I don't disagree."

George wraps up with a few closing bars, then heads back to the bar with Ira, letting himself smile – at least he gave it a shot.

After another round of drinks, Ira heads for the phone at the back to talk business. On the way he runs into Wally Roberts and Fred Astaire.

George sits alone at the bar, drinking a gin and tonic and smoking a cigarette he borrowed from the bartender. His thoughts are elsewhere and a small grin spreads over his face. When he sees the last suitor step away from the gorgeous young woman across the room, he takes his chance. She sets an arm on the balustrade as he approaches, her milk-white skin aglow under the overhead stage-lights.

George strides over, breaking her perfect, timeless portrait. He sidles into view with his cigarette and drink held calmly in his left hand.

"Did you enjoy the show?" he asks.

"Hm?" she says tiredly.

"The show?" George asks again.

"Oh," she says, avoiding his eyes. "I went with friends… Sure, it was good."

"Is it a bit more classical than most?" he asks.

"Well…" She seems to be toying with the conversation, deciding if it's even worth her time. "Wouldn't pass for a French opera. Or any opera, really."

"I couldn't agree more." George takes a step closer. "But I know you heard me playing earlier. The show wasn't that far off, now was it?"

"Ah…" the woman says with a tiny nod. A nod which seems to nullify itself, so you wonder if it was even there at all. "You're George Gershwin."

George smiles. "Guilty."

"Of what?" she asks in an innocent yet seductive manner.

"I," George finds himself at a loss of words. "Well it depends what you consider a crime."

"See?" she says, feigning disappointment. "You're underselling yourself. And you know it."

George smiles and tries to regain his composure. "It's a passing fancy, I promise."

"I promise you're passing on much more," she says, her voice dropping a half-octave in pitch.

George takes this as an advance. "What song serenades you, then?"

She raises a brow, "One that would be commissioned by Ida Rubinstein, that's what. If you're the up-and-coming Gershwin, a man of many talents, then don't you have any interest in composing real music?"

George nods a little too eagerly. "Well, of course. But what do you mean by 'real music'?"

"Gentlemen who invest, like the ones I know, seek artists who chase the ears and eyes of other artists," she says drily. "Not ticket sales. I'd commission a man who could do that a hundred times over. Any old composer can write a few showtunes."

"Well, I focus on the music first," he says. "The ticket sales are a side effect."

She starts to turn away. "Like the other young

composers these days. George Gershwin, as arrogant as *jazz*."

George tries saving the moment, "Wait, wait, wait. Whoever this Ida Rubinstein is... I can ensnare her ear. Where is she?"

"Far," the young woman says, waving at someone she knows and leaving George sputtering for something to follow up with. She's gone in an instant.

A bit dejected, but curious and determined, having heard of this mysterious patron Ida Rubenstein, George goes back to the bar, where Ira is sitting beside Wally and Fred Astaire.

Ira gives Fred a little nudge. "How about George there with his sudden inspiration? Did you like that, Freddie? Was it better than how Kern does it?"

"Sure," Fred says with a smile. "Jerome's an old timer!"

Ira nods. "Well, George can fire out those sorta numbers like clockwork, Fred. But you're a class act. We wouldn't want to insult you with the bottom of the barrel like that. George is capable of so much more."

Wally frowns. "Hey, whaddya' doin'? Nobody talks to Astaire like that!"

"Freddie knows how to take George," Ira says. "He's an artist, Freddie's an artist; we're all artists, here! We express ourselves openly. We speak the same language."

Wally scoffs. "Well I ain't seen much *art* coming out of George lately."

George cuts in and in a cheery voice and says, "When I come back from Paris, that's when you'll get your art." He winks at Ira. "Like he said, I can write for the upper crust."

Wally shakes his head. "Uh-uh. No, no, no. You're not going to Paris. That's only going to set us back."

George ignores him and goes on. "I need my cup refilled, Wally. Paris is the trick. The culture, the music, the art, the women. It'll be the breath of fresh air I need."

Wally shakes his head once more, "Don't get precious, George. I don't want you waltzing back from Paris with Rhapsody in Cordon Bleu. Look... it's a good idea, but let's do it after the show's safe and bringing in the dough. Art for art's sake, money for God's sake!"

George stares Wally down as Ira fidgets nervously. A waitress brings some drinks over.

"You'll see…" George looks up to see if the mysterious woman is still at the bar – but she's gone.

Something in his head switches and he turns to the waitress, still holding their drinks.

"Hey…" He asks, "Can you tell me where the alluring lady who was holding court has vanished to?"

"You mean, Janus? You just missed her, something about being late for an important art exhibition!"

"Janus… Yes Janus!" George now has a name to work with.

"You gotta talk to your brother, Ira," Wally interjects loudly. "You guys are two weeks late with the songs. I keep making excuses for you, but this show opens next month come hell or high-water…"

"There's no problem here, Wally. Trust me," Ira says.

Within moments, George is rubbing the

waitress's bare feet.

Ira continues talking as he watches George, "I think his eclectic taste will mesh well… I suggested Paris three years ago. Remember?"

"What?" George asks as he smiles at the waitress.

"Straight after 'Rhapsody In Blue', and you thought you knew it all," Ira confirms.

"I wasn't ready. I'm ready now," George says, and turns towards the waitress once more, "Is that good, have I got it?"

Ira throws his hands up in the air "Okay, George, can I have a private word with you? Seriously, now."

George whispers to the waitress. She puts her shoes on, gives him a knowing smile, and leaves.

As George and Ira walk past the bar, Ira speaks, "Listen, we're running late. This is our job, George. If you wanna live like we do, you gotta play the game."

"I'm playing the game. Look, I'm dry Ira, this doesn't stimulate me anymore. I want to go to Paris. I want to indulge in my art…"

"You want to indulge in women," Ira corrects

George.

"No! I'm just not like that. You want a bigger house. We all have our foibles. But I want to write something timeless."

"So," Ira says, "when you've grown a beard and you've turned into a fancy classical composer, what am I gonna do? Write your biography?"

"Once that's out of the way, we can write Friday Night Specials for the rest of time. It'll be easy. But right now, the lightweight musical-review fare is in my way," George declares. "Besides, this will be a chance to get started on that play you keep harping on about!"

Ira rolls his eyes and struts back to Wally, full of bravado.

George watches as Ira gets Wally nodding with a few choice words.

Wally waves over to George. "You gonna shaft me up the ass? Or am I gonna shaft you up the ass for breach of contract? I can always call up Jerome Kern…"

George walks over with a confident smile. "So where do we pick up the tickets for Paris?"

Wally opens his arms in resignation. "Okay

George! Enough! Paris it is." He waggles a finger. "But the deadline doesn't change."

"Well, I guess that's that," George gives Wally a perfunctory nod and walks away.

"He's completely ambivalent," Wally sighs.

"And he's a complete genius," Ira adds.

It does not take long for George to find the waitress he had been talking to earlier. Within minutes, he has her pressed up against a wall in a dark corner, where they kiss and canoodle until she takes George to the back, where she clocks out and they head off into the night in each other's arms.

CHAPTER 3

Two weeks later, George and Ira get on a plane to Paris. George looks impatient, as if waiting for two weeks was the most draining thing he ever did. But when he sets foot on the plane, his spirits swell. He jauntily walks down the aisle, giving eyes to all the stewardesses, tossing his bag into the first open compartment.

"I'm going near the wing, come on," Ira says, sliding past George and deeper down the aisle.

"Ira," George sighs bemusedly, "if we crash, we all die together. Your seating position is irrelevant."

"Shut up," Ira says, letting the claustrophobia and phobia of planes get the better of him. "If you're not looking for the safest seat, will you just roll me a cigarette, please?"

"Another one?" George chuckles. "You just had one at the gate."

"If you don't wanna give me a spasm, just shut up and roll me a cigarette." Ira is still looking for a window seat near the wing, but the rows have filled quickly. At last he spots one. "Look there, with a middle seat for you. Can we just get settled in, now?"

Ira looks back, seeing a few other boarding passengers giving the brothers looks down their noses for holding them up.

Ira hugs his small bag to his chest and slides past the gentlemen in the aisle seat brusquely. The man grunts a little, bending his knees to let him through.

"Come on George," Ira motions him over. "We can have a proper conversation here."

"Maybe you're the one who needs to shut up," George says, eyebrows up.

"Don't be crude," Ira says distractedly. "Oh, did you pack enough suits?"

"What kind of question is that?" George frowns. "You're my older brother, not my mother."

Ira buckles his seatbelt, ignoring the comment. "So, which suits did you bring?"

"I got a new one," George says.

Ira pulls out his tobacco pouch and begins rolling his own cigarette. "Oh yeah, where from?"

George slides into the middle seat, then slips his bulky travel-bag under the seat in front of him. The gentleman in the aisle seat clears his throat to assert himself, looking glad to see the brothers finally settled.

George retrieves his bag from under the seat, setting it on his lap and shows Ira his new paisley suit pants, neatly folded. "I had a new friend help me pick it out."

"It's fine I suppose," Ira says. "A bit garish, but okay."

George smiles. "Another admirer. She just showed up at our doorstep. Wanted to go shopping, and later we helped each other to a 'good luck' Paris send off."

Ira rolls his eyes. "Charmed, I'm sure. What I'm even more sure about is you *not* pursuing her. You have your fun in Paris, but remember who's footing the bill. The deadline is *not* changing, like Wally said. While you're having your little fun, I think I'll try to get started on *Porgy and Bess*."

George turns to his brother dramatically. "Ah? Is this a more confident man beside me now?"

Ira lights his cigarette. "If Hollywood is going

to take us seriously, we need to write something that'll really captures their imagination."

"All right," George warns. "Don't get cocky now."

"Being full of yourself in Hollywood is just a way of blending in," Ira says. "And the silver screen is the key to legacy now. It's no secret."

George shrugs, thinking it's better to let it be. For now, he has what he wants: A ticket to Paris. And besides that, a particularly stunning stewardess walks down the aisle, making sure the last of the passengers are settled. She winks and George. He tips his derby hat in return, and Ira is happy enough to have to last word.

Ira falls asleep soon after the first meal is served, and later that evening, while the plane soars high above the clouds and night sky, Ira leans onto George's shoulder, even though he has the window seat. George shrugs him off and Ira mumbles a drowsy protest, but rolls up his jacket and nods off again, this time against the window.

Free of his brother's drooling head, George takes out the score of Maurice Ravel's 'Le Tombeau De Couperin'.

He flicks on the overhead reading light, and begins to whisper to himself. "If 'By Strauss' didn't get me Janus, then Ravel will teach me how to win her ears."

George reads over the music notes, allowing the melody to dance and flutter in his head. When he reaches the last page, he lets his eyes shut for a few hours. A stewardess comes by and flicks off his reading light. She gives him a look like he's one of the most modestly handsome men she has ever seen, then mutters to herself something about American men. Soon enough, the sun comes up over the horizon, and the plane makes its last curve over the hazy blue morning in Northern France, before it begins the final descent to Charles de Gaulle airport. George stirs when the first beams of sunrise slash through the window, then, when the Ravel score slips to the floor from his lap, he jolts awake.

He reaches down carefully, smoothing the composition as if it were some artefact whose pages could tear or be damaged in the wrong lighting. He tucks the pages back into his bag, while a slow smile breaks over his face. The flight attendants serve each passenger a coffee and croissant. Taking his black, George savours the light breakfast. His eyes sparkle with anticipation and excitement tugs at his heart.

***

Outside by the taxis, cars and buses, George frowns as he tries to put American coins into a pay phone. Ira comes out, huffing and puffing a little with the weight of their checked luggage.

George turns back to Ira. "Can't seem to get this damn thing to work. Not even a way to ring the operator."

"It can't be all that difficult," Ira laments. "I should've sent *you* to get the bags…"

A tall, aristocratic woman, Madame Du Vollé waits nearby. When she hears the pitch and cadence of their decidedly American squabble, she perks up and walks over with the elegant grace of a duchess.

"Can I help you at all?" she asks with a friendly, yet condescending smile.

George looks the woman over, even before

he considers her age barring their compatibility. "How does a fella get a cab around here?"

"Where is it you want to go?" Du Vollé asks gently.

"I'm not sure if you'll know of it," George replies. "We're staying at Maurice Ravel's chateau."

"Et bien! Monsieur Ravel is my dear neighbour. After I've called my mother, I'd be happy to give you gentlemen a lift."

George and Ira happily agree. After a few cigarettes, while Du Vollé makes a lengthy call on the payphone, they follow her to her motor car. George sits up front. Ira takes the backseat, with the luggage piled beside him. With every left turn, he must raise a hand to keep a small briefcase belonging to George from sliding from the top of the stack onto his head.

George stares out the window at the passing Parisian streets, enamoured at his surroundings.

Offhandedly, he addresses Du Vollé, "Is there a good train station where you could drop my brother? You know, with plenty of connections?"

Since all the windows are open, and the city is loud and alive with the morning rush, Ira legitimately can't hear what's being said up front. "What?" he shouts.

"He's very excited to have some time alone," George continues to Du Vollé.

"What?" Ira asks again, leaning forward as Du Vollé takes another left, and the briefcase narrowly misses Ira's head. He shoves it back on top and leans forward again.

"Yes, of course," Madame Du Vollé says, we'll drop him at Gare du Nord. It's not far out of the way." She seems to like George enough to assume he's the leader of the two brothers, and should be the one to answer to, at least as far as their travel plans. "Is your brother not staying at the chateau?"

"I can't hear you!" Ira shouts again over the car horns, street hawkers and sirens.

"Well," George says, deciding it's best to actively remain oblivious, "Ravel only made arrangements for the *one* composer. So, he only thinks I'm coming. It was something of an executive decision, I suppose."

"Well, Monsieur Ravel can be quite picky about who he wants to entertain," Du Vollé warns.

George nods. "So I've heard. And anyway, I think Ira will love stumbling about Paris by himself." At last George turns back to face Ira. "It should give you just the inspiration you've been wanting to get going on your play. Don't you think?"

"Are you casting me off already then, brother?" Ira asks, genuinely feeling left out.

"It's Paris, Ira! It needs to be seen from a personal point of view It's a place where one's own opinions must be formed!"

"Blackballer…" Ira mutters, sitting back as the car veers left, and he flinches to avoid the falling suitcase. This time he doesn't pick it back up from the floor.

George makes a tutting noise and turns back to continue talking to Du Vollé.

"You're ashamed that I can't cut the pedagogy?" Ira murmurs to himself, at the same time excited to have some peace and quiet to enjoy the city. But he knows if he acts disappointed, he will have a bargaining chip with George later.

Du Vollé drops Ira off at the station, where he takes out half the luggage and bids a friendly farewell. By then, the brothers have calmed down, and although George knows he will answer for it later, at least for now the implicit understanding is for both to enjoy Paris, each in their own private manner.

CHAPTER 4

Maurice Ravel, a petite, middle-aged Frenchman sits at his piano in his drawing room, composing. His silver hair is slicked back, but a rebellious strand falls over his wrinkle-strewn forehead and into his eyes. He brushes it back with a toss of his head, peering down his nose at his composition book, jotting a few notes, then hunching back over the keys, where the unruly strand of silver hair falls again into his eyes.

His personal assistant, Aimée Klimeq, appears with a selection of neckties. Ravel is half dressed and heavy-lidded, as if he suddenly awoke from an inspiring dream and had to rush to the piano to put the melody down.

Aimée is in her late twenties, with her black hair neatly pinned and curled. She has clear green eyes and an excellent complexion. Her movements are sure and confident. Aimée is a woman who gets what she wants out of life, she is also a sharp judge of character. She makes her own way, doesn't take advice from bad eggs, and if she must compromise, she makes it play to her advantage at the same time.

"Maurice," she asks, "which ones go in the bag for Berlin?"

Ravel waves her off. "Aimée, you choose. Don't bother me with that trifle now."

Aimée starts to leave as Ravel starts playing again, but he stops suddenly and spins on the piano stool to face her.

"Aimée, wait a minute," Ravel declares.

She turns to face him with a knowing smile, ready for whatever ridiculous demand he's cooked up.

"Listen to this…" Ravel begins playing again. Over his shoulder, he asks her, "Do you hear that? Listen! Do you hear something wrong?"

"No," Aimée says.

"Listen!" he shouts, stopping her in her tracks again. "Click-click-click!" he calls out over the mezzo forte measure he's playing. "Don't you hear that clickety-clacking? I can't play with that racket!"

"Maurice," Aimée sighs, "What are you talking about?"

"My nails!" Ravel exclaims. "Fetch me the scissors! They've been growing *much* faster, ever since you started filing them instead of cutting them like a proper man deserves!"

Aimée shakes her head. "I started using the file because you threw the scissors away. They were too blunt, you said, and you were the one who asked for the file. Said something about a 'man of your station' needing a little more pampering than average. And it was my file, by the way. I had to get a new one!"

"Aha!" Ravel cries playfully. "So, you admit my nails are a menace?"

Aimée crosses her arms. "They do grow quickly."

Ravel goes back to playing. "Well it's settled. Only thing for the disconsolate beasts is to clip them down to the nubs. There must be another pair of scissors. Perhaps one for your hair?"

Aimée turns to leave and mutters under her breath, "You don't hire me as a manicurist!"

Ravel leans back to her as she leaves, his hands flitting gracefully over the keys. "And don't forget, Aimée! It's the blue tie! That's the one I need for the trip. None of the others are important. The cornflower blue one! Aimée?"

But Aimée is gone, and Ravel shrugs, going back to his pattern of playing a few notes and scribbling them down in his book.

Presently, Aimée comes back in, carrying the morning post and a pair of scissors. Ravel finishes writing in a measure.

"There we are," he says, with buttery self-satisfaction, and turns to regard Aimée.

"You have a letter," she says, sorting out the mail on a cherry-wood table.

"Well go and open it, then," Ravel says, getting up from the piano and sitting down at the table. "I'll read it while you cut my nails…" Ravel extends his right hand and holds the letter open in his left.

Aimée takes up his hand and carefully starts cutting the already close-cropped fingernails.

"Ah," Ravel says, and his fingers curl with a little gasp. "It's from the Conservatoire."

Aimée jumps a little, then glares with

frustration. "You have to hold still, Maurice. I almost just cut off your finger."

Ravel looks flabbergasted. "But how can I react with anything but shock and despair?"

Aimée rolls her eyes and puts the scissors down.

"Listen to this," Ravel continues. "It's absurd. They want me to give up a whole day to entertain George Gershwin... It's like blackmail. I am not some schoolteacher! Why should this American, who I'm sure is in love with *jazz*... Why should he get my precious time?"

Aimée looks grateful for the outburst that has jumped to the front of Ravel's mind. Most likely, he's forgotten all about the nail-clipping.

Ravel goes on complaining. "They really take liberties with me, you know?"

Aimée begins sorting the last few pieces of mail. "They commission new works and do all the promotion. So, they expect something in return."

"He's due to arrive on May 21st," Ravel says tiredly. "Oh, what a shame... We'll be in Berlin."

"Maurice," Aimée frowns, worrying like she often does now that her employer is finally losing his mind in earnest. "May 21st is *today*. We don't leave for Berlin until tomorrow."

"Today? George Gershwin is here today, you mean?" Ravel stands up in a tizzy. "No. I can't teach him a thing. Rudimentary chromatic theory would overtax him. Maybe he wants to learn how to extend a piece of music longer than three minutes?" Ravel begins to sweat, looking around for some pressing matter to attend to.

Aimée chuckles, "Wouldn't hurt you to meet him. What else have you got to do today?"

Ravel spins up a random excuse. "I was going to ride into town to buy legumes, it's market day." Ravel goes to the wall opposite the window and starts reaching for an antique bicycle on a pair of wall pegs.

"Marianne already went this morning," Aimée points out.

"Marianne can wash the floors and launder the sheets just fine, but as far as produce goes, her eye for freshness leaves *much* to be desired! If I want something done properly," Ravel says in a fluster, "then I must do it myself. I cannot simply hire out when a difficult task comes along."

"What's difficult about buying legumes?" Aimée asks, her tongue *very* much in cheek.

Ravel ignores her and begins struggling with the bicycle, which may as well have been rusted to the wall at this point.

"And besides," Aimée points out, "you never even ride that thing. Please don't go and hurt yourself just to avoid a little hospitality. It'll be good for you."

Ravel struggles with the cumbersome bicycle and almost topples over as he at last lowers it safely to the ground. The tyres are a little flat, but the heavy thing isn't completely un-rideable. "Look," Ravel says, "these Americans, they aren't *real* people. I'm like real people – who smell like reality and the earth and work! Not like Coca Cola, big cigars and petroleum! I'm someone who shops for his own legumes!" Ravel lets go of the bike to make a sweeping hand gesture, and it crashes to the wooden floor behind him. He gives a little shriek and hobbles out of the way.

Before Aimée can make another comment, he picks up the bicycle and ambles out to the courtyard, red in the face but determined to prove his point.

Out in the morning sun, half-covered by puffy clouds, Ravel narrows his eyes at the trusty steed of old.

"You know what they say," he tells himself. "You never forget how…"

He saddles up on the bike, grunting and panting as he gets the rusty gears going. He wobbles his way through a stone archway and into the street, where Madame Du Vollé's car suddenly appears, heading straight for him. Ravel is watching the cobblestones, trying to avoid the most serious potholes, then looks up at the last second and pulls on both the brakes. Du Vollé lays on the horn, while Ravel gets his Gallic knickers bunched up on the front crossbar, barely able to find his feet on either side of the bike before jumping off the teetering rust-trap entirely.

"Hey! Frenchman! Scurry off!" Gershwin yells from the passenger seat as the car screeches to a halt. But when Ravel spins back to his full stature with a little hop, he realises who it is.

"My goodness," he says to Du Vollé, who doesn't look surprised in the slightest. "The effeminate hat," he says, quickly rushing out of the passenger door. "I hardly recognised you, Maurice Ravel!"

Ravel brushes off his topcoat and gives George a curt little nod. "Ah, Mr Gershwin, yes, of course. I was… just heading out for a moment and hoping to be back before you arrived. We were expecting you later in the afternoon… Well I hope you had a good trip. Come on then, let's get you settled in. Bags?"

"Of course," George says, following Ravel like a lost puppy, but turning back to first give thanks to Madame Du Vollé. "I'm so very grateful, Madame," he says, kissing her hand, then both of her cheeks. "Thanks a million."

"Well," she says, "it was no trouble. I guess some Americans *do* have manners."

George winks. "Yes, Madame. Some of us are *very* well-mannered and *very* well versed in all *manner* of things."

"Oh… my… Arrête!" she says, blushing. "I'm sure I *don't* know what you mean."

George beams, grabs his luggage from the back and gives her a little wave as he hurries to catch

Ravel, who's pushing the bike lamely across the courtyard. Madame Du Vollé gives a swoon and a fluttering glance to George, then glares at Ravel's back as she pulls up the drive. "Hmph. Didn't even thank me for delivering his charge," she mutters under her breath. "Ornery old hat."

George shuffles up to Ravel, who turns back absently and gives a little nod, as if to say, *I'd help with your bags, but I've got the bike, see?*

"Well your neighbours certainly are nice," George says brightly. "Gave me a ride all the way from the airport."

"Indeed," Ravel says. "She's very kind to strangers that can offer her something…"

George smiles, taking this as a compliment.

Annoyed at Gershwin's misinterpretation, Ravel changes tack. "Well, if you make best friends that fast, no wonder you get nothing done…"

George lets this roll off his back and stares with joy up at the frieze of the impeccable old stone working, with little angels and cherubs the whole way around, and the bust of Saint Genevieve beside the side entrance. Ravel rolls the bike inside with a squeak, kicking hard at the kickstand to set it up in the hallway. George follows in through the mahogany double doors, finding himself in a draughty hallway.

Ravel takes George into the first-floor foyer, where the main staircase looms and leads to upper quarters.

"Just leave the bags there," Ravel says. "I'll have them brought up to your room. That is, if you'd like to stay the evening here?"

"Of course, Monsieur Ravel," George says, brimming with gratitude. "I'd be honoured."

Ravel nods and takes George down another hallway with low-ceilings, meanwhile doing his best to hide the limp in his step from his near-fall in the courtyard. Ravel tosses a few pleasantries over his shoulder, explaining the care which he's taken to keep the chateau fitted with modern fixtures, while maintaining the historical standard of restoration. "C'est bon," Ravel says. "This must be a change from New York City, Monsieur Gershwin."

"My God! The streets, the people, the sights, even the air," George exclaims, marvelling at the handcrafted carvings along the floor runners and mouldings. "There's something inspiring in every moment I've been here! Must be good for the musical brain to live in such a wonderful, tranquil city."

"Music comes from within, Mr Gershwin," Ravel says, leading George into a small sitting room. He motions for George to sit down, then takes a seat in a plush, gilded armchair.

"I agree, Monsieur Ravel. For me it's a heartbeat that accompanies me everywhere, and it flutters in a different way depending on the tempo of the life I have around me." George leans forward, eager for Ravel's reply.

"Mr Gershwin," Ravel says coolly. "Be careful not to impose your own limits. There's enough holding you back as it is. When it comes to *my* work, I am just as inspired when living in the metropolis as I am under the harsh wing of the wilderness. Maurice Ravel is Maurice Ravel. No matter where he is. Every composer is given the same tools; a piano and a song book. What we do with the blank page falls on the shoulders of whoever's at the keys."

George looks impressed, crossing his legs to get comfortable. "I'm sure that's true, Sir. But you see, back at home, my own shoulders are weighed down by far too many obligations. My distractions from *real* work."

Ravel nods. "Well, I'm sure such a distinguished figure as yourself has quite a coterie. You have to be selective with your immediate confidants."

"Well," George sits upright again. "I flew over only with my brother for this trip. No entourage. But Ira… He's really my manager, although sometimes he's more like a shadow I can't shake off, or a whining little insect. I sent him off to explore the city on his own as I knew this work between us required all of my focus."

"How humble," Ravel says ironically, "to accept such a challenge of your own accord. But Ira, he writes your music with you, does he not?"

George shrugs. "He's a word guy. But I don't care about the cheesy lyrics. I wanna write like you. Just the melodies. The real stuff. I need my own Ida Rubinstein!"

Ravel gets up from his chair, straightening his lapels. "What about your 'Rhapsody in Blue'?

Didn't you orchestrate that?"

George stands up as well. "It was mostly my arrangement, and all my composition. But I had some help with it. That's why I'm here, Mr Ravel, to learn about self-reliance from you." George clasps his hands together deferentially and beams at the French master.

Maurice Ravel sighs and signals down the corridor. "We all have to start somewhere, George. Songs are a perfectly respectable art form. For many musicians."

Ravel starts leading him down the hall to the kitchen. The short rest in the sitting room has done him well. His step is sprightlier, and not what George would expect from a man over fifty.

"I agree, for many artists commercial success is quite enough," George says to Ravel's back as they pass a few Pablo Picasso sketches on the dark wooden walls. "But I'm ready for stage two. It feels like 'Rhapsody' was only a kind of dimly-lit beginning for me. Take your career for example, Mr Ravel. When was the last time you wrote a *song* or a *ballad*? 1915, was it? 'Trois Mélodies Hébraïque?' But I need a patron, or a couple of them if that's what it takes, for me to be considered the real thing."

Ravel turns back with a brief glance. "Well, Mr Gershwin, at least you've done your homework."

"I was hoping to make fast friends," George says as they enter the kitchen.

"Indeed," Ravel says. "Shall we have something to eat before we begin?"

"Of course," George says, tapping his temple. "Whatever gets the mind right."

"You'll see that the French have a much lighter appetite than you may be used to." Ravel looks George up and down for the first time. "But at least I can see you haven't let yourself carry any added baggage."

"Well, Sir," George laughs. "Like I said, I have enough distractions as is. To add gluttony to the list might ruin me."

Aimée Klimeq looks up from her paperwork at a small desk by the main window. She rises and steps over to meet George.

"Aimée," Ravel says, "I'd like you to meet Mr Gershwin from the United States of America. This is my personal assistant, Mademoiselle Klimeq.

She is my invaluable second pair of hands."

George steps forward with a slight bow of his head. Instead of shaking her hand, he takes both of them up in his own and half-bends to kiss them. But just before his lips touch her gently tanned skin, George pulls back, as if captivated, or else distracted by the clear set of green eyes which Aimée trains on him.

"Enchanté," George says, looking into the alpine pools of emerald green. "A fine pair of…" He almost says eyes, but realises how forward it might seem, especially as he is aware of the stereotype of the rudely frank American. Instead, he praises Aimée's hands. "Your hands – such beautiful, well-manicured nails." George let's go of her hands with a little squeeze. "If you don't mind my saying so."

Aimée turns the colour of the strawberries in the fruit basket behind her. "Oh, not at all, Mr Gershwin." She gives a little lift of her house dress. "Thank you!"

"Aimée," Ravel asks her quickly. "Would you see to Mr Gershwin's things?"

"Oh, no. There are heavy things my brother

had me pack for some funny reason. Too many pairs of shoes, you know. I couldn't possibly…" George says with chivalry.

"Not your baggage," Ravel says. "I'm sure Marianne has already taken them up to your room. But your coat, and your hat, if you'd like?"

Aimée reaches for George's hat and coat, sliding them off him with a practised hand, before he can protest.

"And Aimée," Ravel says casually, "would you bring us a little something in the music room? I should think George would like to try his hand at one of the finest French pianos in the city."

"Of course," Aimée says with a teasing glance at Ravel. "Marianne has already made a salad from this morning's market produce."

Ravel narrows his eyes for a split-second, but lets it go. "That'll be fine, and bring some pâté along with it."

Aimée nods, tucking George's hat and coat into a side-closet. There seem to be all kinds of hidden compartments in the old chateau.

"Shall we retire then?" Ravel asks George. "Given the rate you've been asking them, I'm sure you have many more questions."

George smiles and goes to tip his hat to Aimée, but seeing as it's gone, he gives her a look of mock surprise, then waves an invisible cap with a deep, melodramatic bow. Aimée giggles and blushes. Ravel is already out of the room, and George winks at Aimée then follows Ravel down the hall.

CHAPTER 5

Emerging from the hallway, which twisted, turned, dipped and rose into a large music room filled with sunlight, the two composers go straight for the twin pianos without a word. Ravel heads for an ebony grand piano beside a bay window. Gershwin sits down at the other piano, a garish baroque-style grand which is facing Ravel's. The opposing instruments are ready to duel.

Gershwin's piano is much older, yet shines with the same polish. It's made of dark walnut wood with visible grains, and trimmed with gold filigree along the open top board. Gilt-scrolled lacing runs down to the casters, matching the red-cushioned piano stool in front, with a gilded inlay along the seat, and legs which bow out like bass clefs with clawed feet. Ravel's piano keys are still covered, but Gershwin's are not, so he beats him to the action, starting in on his own Piano Concerto in F.

Ravel crosses his legs, interlacing his fingers. At first he looks impatient, but then shifts to irritation, and finally to humourless interest as Gershwin finishes the first measure.

Ravel shuts his eyes to enjoy the gentle lead-in, then a wry smile appears on his face. "I've often wondered what Tchaikovsky's blue period would have sounded like…"

"You got me there," George says. "I've thought about the resemblance myself." George plays softer, working the pedal and skipping a note here and there. He's played this piece so many times, he can let his fingers move through it without having to focus. "You know," he continues, "I'm most proud of *this* passage." He slows down the tempo, matching up with the melancholy mood settling in. "If it's any excuse; I'm Russian by extraction."

"You betray your heritage well," Ravel says. "Besides, I was only ribbing you."

"And for you, the hidden heritage you distanced your public appearance from… Spanish, correct?" George asks.

"Aha," Ravel sighs. "You did your research.

Yes, I'm something of an outcast as well. My mother's Basque blood has coloured my music, although I'm not any less French than you are American. Speaking of which, we've got Debussy as a musical forefather," Ravel boasts. "And who is it the Yankees have… Joplin?"

George laughs and finishes a line of music with a flourish, cutting the piece a little shorter than usual. He looks across at Ravel, who's spindly fingers are resting on his own piano keys, his eyes fixed on Gershwin.

"The bottom line," George says, "is whether the music stands up, no matter what the influence may have been or continues to be. And you're telling me it doesn't, does it? The work I've done so far, I mean?"

Ravel leers at him, darting his eyes at the keys, as if planning out what to play in his head before he strikes the first note.

"Hmm," Ravel smirks. "Not a bit of pride, and yet I somehow can't accept your modesty as entirely genuine. You still seek my approval, instead of blindly forging a path which you find to be suitable to your gains. Then you *do* betray your heritage, and not just the Russian extraction."

Ravel starts off with a few notes, like a cautious creature testing the water temperature before it dives in.

"I understand the merits of commercial success. Not only financial security but acceptance in the public eye. But since you seem to equate legacy with making 'real' music, I will do my best to advise you." Ravel starts playing in earnest; a piece which Gershwin does not recognise. His eyes light up with the excitement of this blessing from Ravel.

"You have one instrument lurching in front of another," Ravel says, playing his smooth melodies, blending the overlapping notes with ease. "Like mashing puzzle pieces against each other and expecting them to fit." Ravel introduces counterpoint melodies that break the flow, then tapers them off, back to his lilting bars. "Those jolting, fortissimo parts, they're pretty... but they've got no backbone. Being just the little dashes, they've got nothing to hold them to the body of the melody. Like brittle leaves, swept off in a muddy cascade, when they could be lush and falling with a gentle sort of confidence."

Ravel plays a few bars of 'Rhapsody in Blue', and George defends himself. "But that's loved *and* hated! But first loved!"

"Oh, yes," Ravel agrees. "That's your style. That 'Rhapsody in Blue' fame and respect so many men go to the grave yearning for. It travels well…"

George crosses his arms, ready to dig until he's satisfied. "So then, how does my orchestra not die adrift in the rafters of the show-house?"

"We were talking about musical form," Ravel says amid a flurry of high notes. "Not instrumentation. You need the form before you can compose with an orchestra."

George leans into his own set of keys, and the two titans begin trading lines. To illustrate his point, Ravel plays the wavering instrumentation of Gershwin's Concerto in F.

"But they're linked, aren't they?" George asks, taking over just before the third movement. "Like the bridging sections, are they not enough like those long notes in your String Quartet? First movement, woven in like…"

"All composed at the piano," Ravel assures him.

Gershwin begins the opening passage of Ravel's String Quartet in F major, soon seeing the French master's point. "Okay, I see what you mean. Here, where you've woven the parts together, in my composition they seem somehow... welded. Jumpy, like those damn showtunes. Perhaps they ruined my ear... But these bits and pieces aren't bad by themselves. You can't divorce the form from the content. Where I weld, you weave."

"Now you get it," Ravel smiles.

George shrugs, "Easy enough."

Aimée enters with tea on a tray. She deftly unfolds a small serving table and places the tea. George smiles at her, but she's focused on her work, and seems to have more to do in another part of the house. She gives a small curtsy and disappears down the hall.

Ravel, who hadn't even noticed Aimée, begins to play utter nonsense across the bottom octave. His frustration obvious, he stops with a sudden look at George.

"What was that?" George shudders.

"The other ingredient," Ravel taunts. "Your concerto gets mixed reviews because it's bad."

George frowns, but he's determined to remain strong and not take offence. "Well. You don't have to put it so bluntly."

"Perhaps not, but to echo the truth is often a blunt force," Ravel explains. "I had to enter the Prix de Rome over and over. With uproar after uproar every time I was denied. So much so that it gave itself a new name: 'L'Affaire Ravel'."

George grins. "Then people love you!"

Ravel sighs. "They see what they want to see, hear what they want to hear, and read about whatever the papers want to aggrandise. By now, they expect it. I get uproar when I fail. You get uproar when you succeed." Ravel slides the cover over the keys. "There's a reason I sit here with my back to the crowd."

"What?" George says in confusion. "But why?"

Ravel gives him a serious look, with a drawl to match. "Would you rather have an artistic flop succeed and pay your way? Or... have an artistic triumph that's wildly unpopular and crippling?"

"Unpopular triumph!" George declares boldly, swinging a leg over the side of his piano bench.

Ravel sits back on his own stool and buries his

face in his hands. "Perhaps we should shelve the music theory and go back to game theory. You are only here because mediocrity shined its favour on you. And what a day in the sun it is." Ravel stands up and goes to the tea set, as if he expected it to be there all along. "But put yourself in my shoes: An indifferent reception, a public who shames you with hostility for being artistically brave."

Ravel fills his teacup, then gives George an ironic smile. "Before I got so many commissions and offers, I had to beg for a patron to throw me a bone. And I was so unknown, they looked at me with charity; like they were the ones doing *me* a favour!"

"Well there's no shame in asking the fat-pockets for help," George says with genuine sympathy. "And here I am with a theatre full of aristocrats, who all want to hear more Broadway drivel!"

"Americans," Ravel sighs, raising the teapot to offer George tea.

George gives him a small nod then gets up from the stool. "It's a cultural problem, I agree. Why do you think I'm here? Not to mention Ira, with his golden Hollywood dreams. That snooty bastard..."'

Ravel blows on his cup of tea and takes a tiny sip. "And what does 'Rhapsody' pay?"

"Oh, I don't know," George says, dropping a sugar cube. "Ira's the accountant. I guess a hundred thousand dollars a year."

All sound and motion have come to a screeching halt. Ravel slowly sets down his teacup and gives George Gershwin a withering stare. George looks back into Ravel's burning eyes, trying to make light of his fortune and popularity. The men are at odds with each other, but the confrontation stirs up respect on both sides. Now that Ravel knows the number attached to his fame, George isn't sure that his idol will ever show him his secrets. George tries to show deepest modesty in his eyes, and his genuine desire to eschew the gleam of fortune. He knows that Ravel can show him 'true' composition, but the teacher will have to be willing.

Meanwhile, Ravel is even more impressed with George, knowing the dollar-amount of impact he's made so early on in his career. George is relieved to see the frustration and bafflement empty from Ravel's glare. The French master's eyes begin to soften and twinkle, while his cheeks flush with good humour, not to mention the hot tea.

"A hundred thousand?" Ravel shakes his head. "I should be taking lessons from you!"

***

Later that evening, the composers dine on tartine as an appetiser for the main course, roasted duck with red wine jus. The wine keeps flowing and Ravel's already unfiltered mind loosens further, his incisive opinions coming fully to the fold. Gershwin listens with bright eyes and inquisitive ardour. By the time the duck has been polished off, Ravel seems to tire of hearing his own voice, and turns to Gershwin with a questioning gaze.

"This *jazz*," Ravel says. "Apparently your latest influence, no?"

"It's fascinating," George says. "The improvisation, the use of the brass and the reeds… like never before."

Ravel frowns, dabbing at the corners of his mouth. "Well, I've yet to be convinced it can sustain a composer's interest. Do you see yourself doing that for your whole career?"

"Not exactly," George says, his eyes on Aimée as she clears up their plates. "But it's folk music, Maurice... the people's music."

"Mmm... but I doubt if it has the richness, or depth of colour of a more established folk music."

"C'mon Maurice," George says after a sip of wine. "Ancient Negro Spirituals are no different from your Greek or Hebrew folk music."

"My earlier works, though steeped in the distant past, were chanson in the French tradition. Jazz may be the fashion of the day, but I'd like to see you develop as an artist. Carve out your own niche."

Having cleared the dishes, Aimée sits down to a plate of her own. She gives George a small smile, with a look that serves to apologise on Ravel's behalf for his harshness and ineptitude as a host.

"Bon appétit," George says to her in a terrible French accent. Then he looks at Ravel. "Okay. I'll concede on that point. But do you know what that means?"

"What?" Ravel asks, taken aback by Gershwin's

abrupt tone.

"It means I need a teacher! Someone who's done what you're talking about. Someone with a legacy of sound that's all their own. Let's cut the fine words and get down to the nitty-gritty. What I need is my own Ida Rubenstein—"

Ravel bangs the table and the room falls silent. Aimée drops her knife in surprise, looks between the two men then back down at her plate. She mutters something indistinct in French, then glares at Ravel, who's keeping his eyes locked on George.

"No," Ravel says. "This visit is temporary. I am not trained as an instructor, nor do I want to be. Need I repeat myself?" Ravel asks nastily.

George is still not ruffled by Ravel's outburst. He looks around at the tile walls. "The acoustics in here are surprisingly fantastic!"

Ravel looks quickly to Aimée, who's focused on eating. "Now that the matter is closed, let's have another drink," he says, then begins filling up everyone's wine glasses. Pausing at George's glass, he fixes him with a cold, cautionary stare.

The men return to their discussion of music, but steer clear of their careers for a while. Ravel brings up

Les Six, a group of composers working together in Montparnasse. They consisted of Darius Milhaud, Francis Poulenc, Arthur Honegger, Georges Auric, Louis Durey and Germaine Tailleferre. Ravel finds their camaraderie impertinent and uninspired, and speaks to George of their music as empty and downright annoying. He tells George that this merry band of young savants is merely a sign that the end of pure, classical music is well-nigh. Just after the second bottle of wine is gone, Aimée takes her leave. After washing her own plate, she says goodnight to George, sweetly. She turns to Ravel with a much colder adieu, as if speaking to a child who has rudely misbehaved.

Instead of trying to assuage her, Ravel waves her off distractedly. "Goodnight, Aimée. Yes, yes, and thank you for the dinner."

Once Aimée is out of sight, Ravel drinks the dregs of his glass and stands up. "Now, Mr Gershwin…" He sweeps his hand over the empty wine bottles. "As you can see, we're in need of more wine."

George gets up, pretending to sway as he does. Ravel doesn't even notice the joke, instead making a beeline out of the kitchen and through a side door George hadn't noticed before. Outside in the darkness, George sees Ravel walking quickly across the lawn, moving much faster than he remembered. Squinting in the dark, he mutters to himself in surprise, then stumbles down the steps after Ravel.

***

The chateau grounds are swathed in shadow and pale moonlight. George must hurry to catch up to the French master. "You were saying, earlier…" George asks, "about Les Six?"

"Don't go bringing up that pack of degenerates," Ravel says bitterly. "Are you trying to see me off on purpose? Well, anyway, now you've done it. They're like malnourished calves suckling on my creative udders. Forget them, Mr Gershwin. You've got nothing to learn from that insolent *cercle secousse.*"

George falters slightly, confused at the sudden burst of French. "Well, where is it you're going then, Sir?" he asks, trying to sound humble.

"I'm getting us some good wine," Ravel mutters, barely audible, then resumes his bustling pace, heading for a farmhouse across from the chateau.

"Les Six," George mutters, thinking Ravel can't hear him. "That's who I imagined the Paris school would send me to. But I think they were too busy."

Ravel spins round on him, raising a finger to George's astonishment. He waggles it at him in rage and disgust. "Busy! I'll tell you what they're busy doing – pounding away with no sense of direction at the keys. Stuck in their sticky, seedy little *hive*, producing insipid, sugary dross for their Queen Cocteau! Jean Cocteau, the queen of those mindless drones... each of them, indulging in their own rock-bottom arrangements. Truly, it's all in the name of heartless excess! Those poor fellows won't have half a mind left over..." Ravel sighs, composing himself and lowering his finger from George's face. "It's a shame, really, such talent eaten alive at the price of gaudy glamour. Such potential among them, too. All of it putrefied by the vice of poor taste."

George opens his mouth to speak, but nothing

comes out.

Ravel purses his lips, giving him a look as if he still has much to learn. Then he turns to the farmhouse and hurries the rest of the way. "Et voilà, here's the best wine available at this hour." Ravel goes up to a wooden-slatted window and starts rapping. "Henri? Madame Lafarge? *C'est tard et nous n'avons pas des vin! Pardon, Henri!*"

Henri opens the window and peers out with a sleepy look. He's about mid-fifties, blue-jowled at this late hour, and still possessing a full head of thick, dark hair. Even in the moonlight, George can see from his sunburnt nose and cheeks that Henri is a hard labourer. He rubs at his eyes and looks out the window of the modest farmhouse.

Henri nods at Ravel, but his eyebrows shoot up when he sees him with a guest. "Well, Maurice," Henri says, "you've decided it's worth having friends?"

Ravel sneers, irascible as usual. "This one's an American! The Academy forced me to show him a few things about *real* music."

"I see," Henri says, passing George a look of pity. He turns to Ravel. "The usual then?"

"Double it," Ravel says, laying a hand on the small of his back, cringing a little. "I think I might've rushed over here too quickly. Don't want to have to come back."

Henri nods, disappears, then reappears with a gas lantern and six bottles of wine in a spindly wooden carrier. Ravel pays him in paper francs, then leads George back to the drawing room, where he fills up their glasses with pungent red wine. The fire crackles, sending up spikes of flitting shadows. Ravel sips the wine, swishes it in his mouth with decorous pleasure, then goes straight for the ebony grand piano by the window. Tipping George a little wink, he starts in on Gershwin's 'Stairway To Paradise'. George hums along and starts tapping his foot. He reaches for his wine and takes a sip.

George squints and coughs, nearly spitting up. He sets the glass down roughly, spilling a few drops on the tablecloth, which is luckily the same shade of burgundy as the wine. Ravel doesn't notice, but for George it only gets worse. Coupled with the burning at the back of his throat, the bright flames of the fire grow with intensity, to the point that he has to squint to avoid being blinded, even in the low-lit room. Next moment, a high-pitched tone crashes through his headspace, seeming to ring between his temples like a tuning fork. His hands start shaking and he begins rubbing his eyelids, then alternate temples with whichever hand is free. As Ravel plays on, the crushing blow of the panic-headache begins to fade, and George tries to focus on the lilting tones of his own composition – rendered, in fact, quite wonderfully by Ravel.

"Jeez," George mutters, his head finally cooling off. "I should slow down."

Ravel hears him this time, and finishes the measure with a flourish. "You've had but a grape or two!" He beams over at George, then softens his gaze.

"You do look a little pale," Ravel says, crossing his arms.

George picks up his glass of wine again and smells it. "Is this… old?"

"Yes," Ravel smiles. "That's the point!"

"It just smells a little off," George says carefully. "Perhaps *too* fermented."

Ravel glares at George. "You're not impressed?

Don't tell me New York City has better wine than Paris!"

"I just… Well, no," George says, not wanting to upset Ravel again. "I suppose I'm just… adjusting to the flavour." He takes another very small, cautious sip. "It's good!"

"Well, since you've adjusted, it's about time for me to show you something," Ravel says. "Stay here, I'll fetch it."

Ravel gets up, looking excited and devious, then leaves the room, humming the rest of 'Stairway To Paradise'. George sets the wine down and goes to the bar-cart for a glass of water. Moments later, he hears Ravel marching back down the stairs in the hallway.

He appears in the doorway with the broadest grin he was worn for George so far. "You were right to call me a weaver," Ravel says proudly. "Let me show you my most treasured possession." He moves toward George with something held behind his back. "They thought of me as an upstart; a young pretender to Claude Debussy's throne, saying he looked down on me. That wasn't true, although I was in awe of him." Ravel closes the distance to a few feet, bringing out a tatty leather trunk. It's about the size of a bread box, with two brass clasps that look so oxidised they might've crusted shut. "Debussy is the music of France," Ravel says, petting the lid of the travelling case gently. "The fact is that he trusted and respected me." He looks to George as if demanding a response.

"Sure," George says awkwardly. "I can imagine."

"But do you know what I mean by respect?" Ravel asks, his hands shaking a little, gripping the trunk. "Do you know how much he trusted me?"

"No – I..." George says, still reeling slightly from the headache.

Ravel slides the eyehooks out of the clasps, letting them dangle a moment for effect. Then he opens the small trunk and tilts it toward George.

Inside the baize-lined trunk is nothing but a pair of slippers, with suede so faded it's worn through at the toes. The insoles are so yellow and cracked, they look like a dry lakebed.

George looks up from the slippers and meets Ravel's eager smile. Gershwin is unsure what to say.

"That's the sort of trust I'm talking about," Ravel says.

"You mean... these are Debussy's slippers?" George asks.

Ravel simply nods, handing George the travelling trunk. George takes it, peering down at the slippers, then jerks his head from the full force of the stench. George lets go of one of the carrying handles to plug his nose, and the slippers nearly tumble out.

"Careful with that!" Ravel says, yanking the teetering trunk from George's hand. Along with the smell, George thinks of the weight of the late composer's slippers—heavier than expected. But he chalks this up to whatever super-mould is in the slippers, and likely has a colony in the baize-lined box as well.

The French master flicks George a gaze, then carefully shuts the lid and hooks the claps.

George smiles back at him. "Did you think of those when I said the wine smelled bad?"

Ravel stays focused on securing the trunk, setting it on a table as though it's a nuclear-fission explosive. He strokes the lid three times before casting George a condescending glance. "My Lord, you are incorrigible," he sighs. "Yes, in Monsieur Debussy's final years, riddled with cancer, these very slippers allowed him to complete his final works. He was sick for nearly three years, and with that sort of cancer... nobody has beaten it. And aside from their creative power, who knows how much the slippers prolonged his life?"

George tilts his head, interested more in Ravel's alternative belief system than the apparent magic imbued in the slippers.

A sorrowful look comes over Ravel's face, mixed with a measure of fear for his own death. "After his surgery in 1915, he once compared the simple act of dressing in the morning with 'one of the twelve labours of Hercules'. The poor, wonderful man."

George nods sympathetically, his eyes drawn to the travelling trunk again. George Gershwin is struck with the idea that he missed an opportunity to really inspect the slippers. But he quickly pushes the illusory thought from his head.

Ravel drinks deeply from his wine glass on the table. "Anyway, they were his inspiration... and now they are mine. He was never without them when he wrote his masterpieces. I'm not superstitious, nor do I believe in God, but I admit – I've felt their power."

"The smell's black, I'll give you that," George says. "Like burnt tyres."

"That should be no surprise. The man's been dead for six years." Ravel wears the hint of a smile, but he still looks worn-out – as if discussing the death of his idol is draining him.

"So, you wear them now?" George asks, hoping to lighten the mood.

"At first, I only dared to put them on. When I was having a hard time finishing some difficult work. I didn't want to become dependent…" Ravel finishes his glass of wine and sighs. "But now, I can't even start something new without them on."

George gives the French master a curious frown. "They sound more harmful than helpful."

"If it sounds deranged to you, Mr Gershwin, well, that's your problem," Ravel says matter-of-factly. "Either way, their physical nature is beyond a doubt. The slippers of Claude Debussy, bequeathed to me, from the hand of one *humble* composer to another."

George must bite his tongue to keep himself from rolling his eyes. But he wonders if his resistance to believing Ravel's story is in fact the very reason he should believe. *The legendary slippers*, George thinks to himself, wondering whether there could be some truth to the tale. Instead of making another joke, he puts on a serious face and stares at Ravel. "Could I try them on sometime?"

"No!" Ravel screams, swooping the trunk to his chest and hobbling to the foot of the stairs, where he rings a bell for one of his housekeepers. Ravel sets the slippers on the bottom step and returns to George to refill their glasses. His momentary panic seems to fade with the splash of red wine. "I'm sorry," he says to George, "but Debussy gave the slippers to me. For you to wear them would have no effect, and might in fact ruin the magic. Consider yourself *touched* to have seen them."

George tries to ask more questions, but Ravel holds up a hand and purses his lips. George let's it go, and soon enough the two of them are back on the subject of other great composers, drinking wine and going down tangents on theory and music history.

Marianne appears on the stairs, rubbing her eyes. With a quick look at Ravel, she gathers the trunk and heads back upstairs, as if the slipper retrieval was common practice at this hour.

As the wine continues to flow, Ravel passes out on the chaise longue. George is still wired from the whole experience, and the idea of the magic slippers won't be pushed from his mind. Listless, George goes over to a rolling desk and starts looking through it. The desk is full of half-written compositions by Ravel, and George lights some candles to begin perusing them, humming the notes to himself as he happily studies.

Soon enough, Aimée passes the threshold in the hallway on her way down to the bathroom, but she hasn't been sleeping well, so she pauses to watch George at work before going back up. George is so focused, he hardly even notices her watching from the doorway, holding a gas lantern with a guttering flame.

Aimée starts fiddling with the knob on the lantern, watching the flame flicker a few moments. At last George looks up and sees her on the threshold.

"Oh," George says, sliding off his reading glasses. "Aimée, Hi."

"Hi," Aimée echoes.

A moment passes and George's emotions bowl over. "I'm blowing this!" he cries, dropping his head into the mess of sheet music on the desk.

Aimée rushes over, as if she had known the outburst was coming. "No, no, no! Leave this alone for now. It's too late to be worrying so much." She puts a hand on his back and rubs it gently.

George looks up at her, a page stuck to his chin.

She peels off the page, then starts sorting the welter of papers into a single pile.

"But," George says. "They'll be out of order, I—"

"Stop worrying," Aimée says with a hard stare, shutting the desk and pulling him up by the hand. She takes the lamp in her other, then leads George into the hallway, which is pitch dark. Light bleeds from the crack in the door from a spare bedroom, and Aimée leads him to it, into one of the many guest rooms in the chateau.

This room has a fleur de lis wallpaper-pattern, with a cornflower-blue trim along the mouldings, and limestone windowsills wide enough to sit on. Aimée settles George onto the four-poster bed, with a quilt and a pile of feather pillows at the headboard. George slumps back on the bedspread with a heavy breath full of resignation.

Aimée sits beside him. "Mister Gershwin, you mustn't worry. Nobody does well with him, because he doesn't do well with anyone. Maurice's psychology... Well, it's like a God complex mingled with father issues, dropped into that uphill battle with Monsieur Fauré."

George sits up on his elbows. "He studied with Fauré?"

Aimée nods demurely. "At the Conservatoire. But he could never earn respect from that hard-faced man."

George's eyes light up again, this little secret lifting his mood. "You met him?"

"A few times," Aimée says. "And there was no compassion in his eyes, only the drive to compose. I never saw anyone like it. As if he took no pleasure in any other slice of life. I couldn't believe he was French!"

"But..." George is pouting again, still frustrated,

jealous of Ravel for having such a mentor as Gabriel Fauré. "Even if his teacher had run him into the ground with endless lessons. Even if he had made Ravel play until the pads of his fingers grew calloused, he would still be Maurice Ravel! The French master!" George turns to Aimée with a puppy-dog look, taking up her hand with a suave reflex she doesn't resist. The chemistry between them is that fast and easy. "And besides that," George says, "Maurice has the slippers!" He tosses her hand away, then falls back on the bed and hugs a frilly pillow.

"Oh, Christ…" Aimée looks worried. "He's already shown you? Mon Dieú… You know I clip his nails?"

"Oh. Wow…" George rolls over, his mouth agape. "His toenails, too?"

Aimée boxes him playfully in the shoulder. "Stop it. Not his toenails, that's where I draw the line."

George puts his chin in his hand, kicking off his loafers discreetly. They tumble off the side of the bed, and Aimée gives him a look. "You're sleeping here, then?"

George rolls over to look up at the tin-stippled ceiling. He yawns. "I'm not sure, just getting comfortable." He looks back at her with eyes he hasn't shown her yet – half-lidded and filled with affection and desire.

She can't help but smile a moment, then she looks away, finding her reflection in the mirror on the armoire. Her dark hair is long and sleek as a stallion's tail. She's just finished her nightly brushing and lavender-oil treatment. "Well," Aimée says. "That's how bad it is. This man – wonderfully talented, don't get me wrong – he needs to be pampered like a child to create. And he hates the public, which has got him used to not leaving the house at all, walking around the chateau with his robe wide open…"

"Sign me up!" George cuts in. "Sounds like the life for me."

Aimée catches his gaze through the mirror. She shakes her head. "Not me, I need other people."

George sits up. "I need people, too," he says. "But you have to understand how celebrity takes all the privacy you have, and tosses it out the window."

"But you knew that getting into it, right?" Aimée asks.

"Sure," George agrees. "But, Ravel's reclusion–it seems to be his way of working around it. I envy him for that."

"Well, okay, I can see that," Aimée says. "Just don't envy me for having to take care of him. He can be such a monster… Oh, but he can be sweet, too. Sometimes…"

"There's many things I envy you for, but watching over Ravel isn't one of them."

Aimée turns, intrigued. "Really? What are you jealous of?"

"Your eyes, your cheekbones, your lips. The undertones in your accent, like a walking bassline played slow in a smoky bar. Whenever you speak English, it tugs at my heart like that sort of music always does."

Aimée blushes. "My English, is it good?"

"Perfect," George says, looking into her eyes.

"What else?" she asks, toying with him, but sure of where this is going.

George reaches for a strand of her ebony hair. "Your hair, with the French wave, and how you wear it down, not spraying it up like a typical American girl."

Aimée smiles. "I have to work at it, Mr Gershwin. Just like anyone else."

"And that's the other thing," he says. "You are *just like anyone else*, and yet, there's some mystery you're hiding. Like a magical secret that's too wonderful to share with just anyone. That's what I'm jealous of."

Next moment, George moves in to kiss her. At first, Aimée keeps her eyes open, still seeing both their reflections in the mirror. Shortly, she closes her eyes to enjoy the moment.

Then she pulls away, covering her smile with her hand. "You taste like stale wine."

"Courtesy of Ravel," George says with a shrug.

"Is that what the Americans call romance?" Aimée asks. "Kissing whichever girl you're alone with at night?"

George gives Aimée an irresistible smile. Then he shrugs again, even more nonchalantly. "Ravel says that's my problem. I can see all the pretty parts—" He points at the two of them in the mirror, sitting on the edge of the bed, and gestures around like he's counting up their positive qualities. "I can see what's beautiful, put the small things together piece by piece, put them into the music." He turns to her with a downtrodden look. "But I guess I don't connect them right. That's what he says."

Aimée takes his hand. "Don't let him get to you. I think you connect all the pretty things very well. Maurice is… impressive. I understand that. But he has a hard time accepting love, so don't get your hopes up for having him as a mentor."

"That's what I'm coming to grips with," George says with a tender sigh.

Aimée pats his hand. "He'll either come around, or he won't."

"We could say the same for you," George says with a broad smile.

Aimée giggles. "I've already decided about that."

George pulls her into another kiss, and they fall back on the bed, where they spend the rest of the night together. Aimée sneaks back to her bedroom in the early morning. George wakes up with a headache from the wine, and the trace of her lavender oil in his bedsheets.

CHAPTER 6

L ater that morning, Aimée comes down in a pale-yellow sundress with a blue velvet sash. She enters the drawing room where Ravel is still out cold. He's snoring and muttering to himself in his sleep, sprawled out on the chaise lounge, having slept through the night with no pillow or blanket.

"Maurice, you need to pack," Aimée says sharply. Ravel turns over and cracks open his eyes to a squint.

"What? Will you cut the lights, please, it's so early…" Ravel groans.

Aimée goes quickly to the window and draws the curtain. A burst of morning light shines through. Ravel shrieks, pitching off the chaise lounge and scrambling to his feet. His eyes are like red marbles. He's hungover as a wino on New Year's Day.

"Urgh! Aimée! Can't you see I'm sleeping?

Ahhh… my head. Something for my head, please."

"At least tell me what you'd like to pack," Aimée says evenly, still holding impatience at bay.

"Pack…? For what?" Ravel says, flopping onto the chaise again.

Aimée heaves a sigh. "For the train to Berlin. We're leaving this afternoon."

"Berlin?" Ravel sits up and smacks both his hands to his head, covering his eyes and rubbing his temples. "Good heavens! Just pack the slippers, that's all that matters. Have Marianne choose a couple suits, and some casual garments, too, of course. And one of my finest evening sportscoats… she'll know which one I mean." Ravel gets up and wobbles over to Aimée, shielding the sun from his eyes with hands. "But Aimée, whatever you do, please, please pack the slippers. And one more thing! Get a ticket for George Gershwin, too."

"You want him to come with us?" Aimée almost lets out a gasp she's so surprised. "But yesterday you were trying to wriggle out of meeting him!"

Ravel waves her off. "Oh, Aimée, how could one make a judgement on a person without meeting them? You have to give people a chance, you know?"

Aimée's mouth hangs open. She can't believe the hypocrisy, but she knows it's best to let it slide. Ravel shuffles off to the kitchen, muttering about cold water and hot coffee.

***

When Aimée enters the kitchen, she sees Marianne serving George a big pile of fried eggs on toast. As Marianne moves away, George catches her arm. "You know what they call these in America?" he asks. "Sunny-side up. You see? The yolk. Yellow, like the sun?"

But Marianne's English is not good. She smiles apologetically and moves on to serving Ravel, who is now slumped down in one of the high-backed chairs. He waves off the eggs and demands coffee.

But Aimée is at the ready, sliding an espresso in front of Ravel, then sitting down at her own plate. "Mr Gershwin," she says, "how is your breakfast?"

"Very good, thank you. I was just telling Marianne how we call this sort of breakfast 'sunny-side up'."

Aimée winks at George. "We wanted you to feel at home."

Ravel drains his coffee in a single gulp, only pausing briefly to grimace at the heat.

"Maurice!" Aimée says, "You'll burn off your tongue!"

Ravel just mutters something incomprehensible, then rakes away cups and saucers to get to his manuscript at the other end of the table. He starts sorting pages, scanning each line with razor-keen attention. Meanwhile, Marianne finds a small corner of the table to leave Ravel's breakfast, should he ever decide he can manage a couple eggs. Then she sits down to her own meal, a croissant and a coffee.

George turns to Marianne, then Aimée. "Thank you both. But I didn't need some special breakfast. I could've eaten the French way. What would you be having?"

Marianne, who didn't understand a word, just smiles and takes a bite of her croissant.

"Ah…" George says. "But of course. Something light."

Ravel glances at his fried eggs in disgust.

"Light. Yes. Certainly not *this*. If I thought I could stomach anything," he glares briefly at Marianne and Aimée, "I'd be quite upset. But just as well, letting this American excess go cold." Turning back to his manuscript pages, he starts muttering again. "No, no… I don't remember this. What is this?"

Aimée, who's been enjoying the American way for a change, pipes up. "*This* is your breakfast, Maurice. We aren't going to cook something else, and we've got a big day, so you better eat some of it. We don't have time to stop on the way to the train station." George senses the growing irritation in her voice.

"I'm not a mental cripple!" Ravel retorts. "I can see very well what the cowboys get fat on. If you paid much attention at all, you'd see I'm talking about my manuscript." Ravel gathers too many papers up at once, spilling sheets out all over the table. "These are not as I left them! Was there tampering, perhaps… while I was sound asleep?" He glares briefly at George, who doesn't notice. He's too busy sopping up his eggs with a piece of baguette.

Aimée gawks at Ravel, dreading the oncoming travel day. Getting Ravel to the train station without having a breakdown now seems like a terrible challenge. She turns to Marianne with a look of shallow envy, wishing she could stay behind and tend to the chateau. But Ravel has her pegged for any extended outings. While Aimée is stewing, George sniffs deeply. His nose wrinkles and his brows become knotted with sudden concern. Aimée forgets the trouble with Ravel, because George looks cute as a bunny while he keeps sniffing. Even so, Aimée gets a feeling of unexplainable concern, as if George's brain has misfired, and his reaction just now is a kind of delusion. She watches George stand up and go over to the stove top, where he takes hold of the cast-iron skillet on the backburner.

"If you all keep bickering... the onions will burn." Aimée grows more concerned. She was hoping at least George wouldn't need a watchful gaze while getting to Berlin, but the way he's sniffing around for a phantom scent, she has to wonder...

George looks in the pan and sees nothing there.

"Burning," he says, then turns back to the table. Marianne is minding her own, sipping coffee. Ravel is pouring over his jumbled stack of papers, Aimée averts her eyes quickly, making it seem as if she wasn't watching George with concern.

George opens his mouth to speak, then thinks better of it. He could have sworn there was something burning on the stove. He quickly looks out the open window to the courtyard, hoping to see a car running, or some sort of machine to explain the smell of burning rubber. But there's nothing but the birds having a bath in the fountain, and across the lawn, Henri, tinkering with an oxcart in the yard.

"Gershwin," Ravel says, peering over his pages. "I must insist that you let Aimée take care of the cooking."

George starts, then picks up the cast-iron pan, taking it to the sink where he begins to wash the dishes. "Oh, sure," George says, happy to take his mind off his olfactory hallucination. "But I can at least help with the clean-up... If she and Marianne went to all this trouble, it's the least I can do."

"Nonsense," Ravel says. "You offend her."

"None taken," Aimée says, quite impressed with a man who offers to clean.

George returns the wink she gave him earlier. "It's an American thing, you see. The guest must be just as good to the host as the host is to him."

Ravel lets the matter slide, turning back to his manuscript. "Well, I must say it's rather queer for a guest – for a *man* – to be washing dishes. But if she's all right with it, then wash away, *Américain*. She has some good news for you anyhow."

"Oh!" Aimée blushes then covers her mouth. She stands up to help George with drying the clean dishes. "Mr Gershwin, I'm going to book you a ticket for Berlin. I hope this doesn't inconvenience any prior arrangements."

"Berlin?" George's eyes dart around, landing on the mixed-up manuscript pages. "No. Not an inconvenience at all." He turns off the tap on the sink. "It would be my pleasure to… see my teacher in action." He glances at Ravel, who's still grumbling away at the manuscripts. "To see him performing…" George is clearly shocked and nervous at this exciting change of plans.

Aimée smiles a little wider, finding George's

behaviour incredibly endearing. Through his admiration, she finds the old fondness she once had for Ravel.

"To see his whole process come to fruition," George continues.

"With your very own eyes," Aimée says, finishing for him.

"Yes, yes," Ravel nods, "It's all very well for a young composer to see the result of such constant, diligent inspiration. Having the right relationship with the muse… of course that's a good part of it. But also, one must know how to travel, and make room for the muse wherever you may be. So, you might learn a thing or two from the rambling malaise of our travels, and…" Ravel struggles to tie up his pompous, drivelling speech. Searching for the right words, George decides to bail him out. He crosses the room and starts gathering up the remaining pages, still strewn all over the table. "I can take those, Monsieur Ravel. I have my own way of keeping things in order, and when we get there, we can sort it out together. I'm sure you could use the extra hands."

"Well," Ravel says, a rare twinkle in his eyes. "I

couldn't figure how they went in my current state. The wine from last night still has quite a grip on me. Go ahead then." He hands the other stack of pages to George.

"Not to worry," George says, "I'll take care of it." Having gone over the manuscript the night before, George is quite confident he can reassemble the piece, although it might have some of his own alterations slipped in.

Ravel seems to understand that George was in fact the one tampering with the order of the pages the night before, but he won't admit such vulnerability to George or the rest of the room. "I'm not worried," Ravel says. "I'll just need to turn whatever scribbles and notes you make into my own perfection, and I always do. I am quite sure you won't be able to improve it," he chuckles, "but just get it back to a working order. And we still have a few more days until the show."

George smiles. "I'll do my best. We can drum up the final when we get to a piano in Berlin. You'll have the last word."

Ravel taps his spoon on his cup of coffee, and Marianne gets up to refill it from the French press. Ravel sips his coffee, and George slides the untouched plate of eggs over from the edge of the table.

"Come on, Maurice," George says with a jocular grin. "You seem fried. Keep on the sunny-side!"

Ravel waves him off, draining his second espresso. "Just get the pages back in order, and not too many *jazzy* notations, okay? And by the way, just because some crazy *Américain* looks at my composition, doesn't mean I trust him enough to eat this sort of *sloppy* thing for breakfast." Ravel brushes a bit of fried egg off George's waistcoat. "If you stay here long enough, you'll learn what it means to be *refined*."

"That's settled then," Aimée cuts in. "No time to lose, we must be on our way."

"I'll go and pack my things," George says. "Just give me about ten minutes."

"Perfect," Aimée says with a coy smile. "If we have to wait for anyone, it'll be Maurice."

Ravel makes a tutting noise. "I'm fine now, I've had my coffee."

George turns back before leaving the kitchen. "Sorry about the dishes!" he calls out.

Marianne starts clearing the table and waves him off. "T'inquiète pas," she says sweetly, filling up the sink.

George looks confusedly at Aimée.

"It means *don't worry*," Aimée says. "Now go on. We probably won't stay more than a few days, but just in case, bring whatever you need for a whole week. We'll be outside in the courtyard when you're ready."

CHAPTER 7

As the afternoon train for Berlin pulls away from the station, George looks out the window, infatuated with a true sense of romance. The city streets fall off into a golden countryside, and George Gershwin shivers like a schoolboy on a grand vacation.

Gershwin leans into the cool glass of the window, then folds his jacket to make a pillow. There's a bed in the compartment, but he fancies a nap. Just a wink of sleep so he can wake up again and still catch the sunset. He thinks of the scarlet rays of sun painting patterns over the purple dusk. Drifting off, he wonders if he's ever been happier…

"George!" Ravel shouts from the next-door cabin.

For a moment, Gershwin pretends the voice came from a half-dream. But then Ravel's voice rings out again – surprisingly shrill despite being muffled by the wall.

George sits up from the window with a sigh. The sun has gone behind some clouds, and the train compartment is growing chilly. When he opens the sliding door to the corridor, a cool draft runs along it, and George goes for his travelling sportscoat before leaving. The floor of the hallway rattles along the tracks. With a hand on the linenfold-panel wall for balance, George knocks on the door to the cabin beside his own.

"Entrez!" Ravel shouts from the other side of the door.

Inside the cabin, Ravel is stretched out on the lower berth. The upper berth is stuffed with all manner of suitcases, teetering precariously with the sway and pitch of the train. Aside from the train's clattering wheels, the squeak and groan of bedsprings is the only sound.

"Maurice?" George whispers.

A pale hand flits out from behind the sleeping curtain and draws it back. Ravel sits up in the lower berth with a black blindfold over his face, set oddly askew on his clammy face.

George laughs. "You won't see a lick of the country with that on!"

"I've seen it all before! Do you know how many times I've made this trip?"

George considers his answer, but before he can speak, Ravel cuts in.

"Never mind," Ravel huffs. "The train wheel beneath this car has a dreadful click-clucking to it." A moment of silence passes. George doesn't hear anything.

"Can't you hear that?" Ravel asks frantically.

George is still having a hard time seeing past the melodrama. "Take the blindfold off, would you?"

Ravel rips the blindfold off, scowling at George with eyes like chips of ice.

"On second thought…" George murmurs.

Ravel slides his feet out from the bunk. "Switch rooms with me," he demands.

"But, Mr Ravel… I just got everything in there!" George protests.

Ravel gets up and waves his arms. "No bother, just leave your stuff in there! The cars are for sleeping, anyway."

As Ravel throws on a smoking jacket and slides into a pair of loafers, George tries to explain that he isn't ready to sleep yet. "If I don't have my things, what will I do? What can I work on, what will I read?"

George follows Ravel into the corridor, still trying to convince Ravel, who looks back quickly and quips, "You won't have to read. Just look out the window. Like you said, there's wonderful countryside out there. Don't want to miss it."

"But," George tries again weakly, "After it gets dark, I won't be able to see anything."

Ravel has already disappeared into George's cabin. George exhales with a feeling of sheer confusion, but he's getting accustomed to life around Ravel.

"Just along for the ride, I suppose," he mutters to himself, then goes back inside Ravel's cabin. Heading over to open the shutters, one of the precariously perched portmanteaus from the upper berth comes sliding down, nearly whacking him on the head. He catches the small suitcase. It's a tatty leather trunk, about the size of a breadbox. He gives it a cursory glance and tucks it under the lower berth. Too tired to bother with the blinds, he sits down on the bunk, which Ravel left in a mess of tangled sheets.

George starts unbuttoning his shirt and tugging at his necktie, humming to himself as he gets ready for bed.

"And now, yet another night, just another night..." he sings quietly, then stops to chuckle when he hears Ravel already snoring from the other cabin.

***

Meanwhile, Aimée sits in her own bunk, propped up with a pen and her journal. She's got the private sleeping cabin across from Ravel, which is now occupied by George. She's happily setting down the events of the day, when a grinding, metallic noise gives her a sudden start. Knowing what a light sleeper Ravel is, she hurries out of bed in her chemise. On her way out, she pulls on a belted nightgown hanging from a hook by the door. She doesn't bother with shoes, instead padding across the hallway barefoot. She gathers herself with a short breath, then knocks softly on the opposite cabin door.

"Maurice? Maurice, are you awake?" she asks, then knocks again a little harder. The latch slides free, having not been properly shut, and the door swings open on its hinges. The compartment is dimly-lit, the sunlight having faded from the small window, and not one of the lanterns lit. Aimée peers inside, then quickly averts her eyes when Gershwin turns toward her, half undressed.

"Oh Aimée, I'm sorry," George says bashfully, quickly buttoning his shirt back up. "Maurice and I swapped cabins."

Aimée turns to leave. "My mistake, goodnight Mr Gershwin."

"It's okay, I needed some company," George says, having finished getting his shirt buttoned again. Aimée lingers at the door, her hand on the latch.

"I'm sure you need to sleep," she says, then turns back in the shadowy half-light.

"I would if I could," George says. "Have a nightcap with me?"

Aimée shifts her eyes, but George's hapless grin is irresistible. "All right," she says. "It does sound nice. I think I packed some cognac in one of his cases."

"Now you're talking!" George cries.

Aimée pulls one of Ravel's suitcases off the rack, a brocade portmanteau with a tanned-leather trim. "Wait a minute," she says. "Why are you sleeping in here?"

George gets the first of the wall-mounted lanterns alight, then turns to Aimée. "He said there was some kind of noise keeping him up."

Aimée pauses a moment over the portmanteau to listen. "I think I can hear it, too. Well, I'm not surprised. He's a light sleeper."

"Unless he's been drinking?" George asks genially.

Aimée smiles. "Right. Well, I hope it's not a problem with the undercarriage."

George gets the other lantern lit. "Oh, I'm sure it's not. It sounds like it's coming from next door, not below."

Aimée passes George a bottle of cognac from the portmanteau, then latches the suitcase and slides it back atop the rack. George gets a couple of glasses from the glass-lined cabinet about the basin, then pours a few fingers of the syrupy liquor into each glass.

Aimée sighs. "I'd rather him not have another reason to complain tomorrow. I'd better bring him some earplugs."

George passes her a glass.

"Santé," Aimée says, raising her glass.

"Santé," George says, returning the cheers. "A man like Maurice… He must have his own set of earplugs."

"Of course he does," Aimée laughs. "They must be in here somewhere."

"Go on, have a look," George says. "I'll hold your drink."

Aimée hands him her glass. "Thanks, Mr Gershwin."

"Oh, Aimée," George smiles, "Haven't we moved past such formalities?"

Aimée shoots him a coy smile. "I suppose so. George, then."

"Thanks for having a drink with me," George says. I haven't been in a sleeper car in years. Hopefully I'll get a couple hours…"

Aimée takes down another one of Ravel's suitcases and opens it. "I can't sleep on trains either. I was up reading, that is until that noise disturbed me."

"Try sleeping on an aeroplane," George says, sipping his cognac.

"I can't imagine," Aimée says, too excited to search for the earplugs. "But isn't it peaceful up there? You've done it quite often?"

"I've flown more than a few times, but it isn't my favourite way to go. Tends to turn my stomach," George says, handing Aimée her glass again. "Maybe we can get Ravel over to the States. I'm sure he would take along his travelling companion."

Aimée blushes. "Oh! I'd love to see New York. More than anything."

"And that's how I felt about Paris," George smiles, then changes the subject. "Anyway, what have you been reading?"

"To tell you the truth," Aimée says with some hesitation. "I was actually *writing*."

George's eyebrows go up. "No need to be sheepish! Go on, then. What sort of writing?"

"It's not so easy to talk about," she says. "I'm not an artist like you or Maurice. So, the writing is really just for me."

"Like a diary?" George asks.

Aimée nods. "But I don't make entries every day. I just put down the important events."

"Publish it," George says, raising his glass to his lips. "Sounds like a bestseller. 'Life with the great Maurice Ravel: *An emotional rollercoaster'*."

Aimée laughs and takes a sip of cognac. "That's right – With trauma on every page! Oh, but I couldn't possibly. It wouldn't have any mass appeal…"

George puts on a serious face. "Well. I'd read it."

Aimée narrows her eyes and fixes George with a taunting smile. "You want to read my journal? I'm not sure that's a good idea." She leans against the bunk and looks up at him.

George takes a small step toward her. "And why not? If you knew me better, you'd know I could be trusted."

"I trust you," Aimée says. "But I'm not sure how you'd react to the most recent entries…"

"Something's been inspiring you lately?" George asks.

"Maybe," Aimée says, then studies the pattern in the moquette carpet.

"You don't think I can handle it?" George asks, hoping for more of a reaction.

"You have no idea..." Aimée says, upturning her eyes, then flitting them back to the floor again.

"An intelligent woman's thoughts on a brash New Yorker?" he asks.

"Something like that," Aimée says. "But replace 'brash' with 'talented'."

George smiles and takes another step toward her. Aimée's chest rises, and like a flower turning to the last of the evening sun, she lets herself be drawn in.

"Well, Aimée," George says softly. "I'm flattered. But... I'm no Ravel."

"That's true," Aimée breathes. "You and Maurice are *very* different."

George takes up her free hand. "And *you* know Maurice very well."

"What's that supposed to mean?" Aimée pulls back a little, scooting down the bunk and away from George.

George hesitates, then tries to explain. "I wasn't

implying anything. It's just… You live together."

"And?" Aimée asks.

George considers his next words carefully, as if tasting them to make sure they aren't poisonous. "Well," he says at last, "don't people talk?"

Aimée shrugs. "They may. Let them. I'm not interested."

"So," George says, "do you ever feel stuck? Out on the edge of Paris in the chateau all alone?"

"It's true that Maurice hardly entertains, but I have Marianne. And besides that," she winks, "I'm not always alone. Speaking of which, I don't want you to get the wrong idea about what's happening between us. I mean, you kissed me first."

"Still glad I did," George says. "But there's no obligation to kiss me back."

"I'd like to, sometimes." Aimée says, sidling up to him on the bunk. She kisses him lightly, then pulls away when he reaches for her waist. "Wait, wasn't I looking for something in here?"

"The earplugs," George laughs.

"Check the nightstand," Aimée says. While George searches the nightstand drawers, Aimée reaches atop the luggage rack, stretching to her tiptoes. She pulls down the weathered travelling case, pulls back at the musty smell exuding from it, then sets it on the lower berth to open it. George isn't having any luck searching the nightstand, but he keeps looking diligently, taking intermittent sips from his cognac glass.

Aimée opens the travelling case to find Debussy's slippers. She waves a hand in front of her face and coughs a little.

George turns to her. "What's wrong?"

"Nothing," Aimée mutters. "I just can't believe he's still lugging these awful things around."

George catches a glimpse of the slippers, just as Aimée is shutting the lid and fastening the clasps on the small leather trunk. "Oh, those dingy slippers," he sighs. "Maurice seems to think they have special powers."

Aimée puts the trunk back on the edge of the luggage rack, she turns back to George before she slides it safely to the back. "He told you his theory, then?"

"Oh yes. He's rather fascinated with that old pair of slippers. It's spooky if you ask me," George says, refilling both their glasses. "If anything, they might be haunted, but I don't know about any kind of magical abilities they might be imbued with."

"Me neither," Aimée says, making the cuckoo sign with her finger at her ear.

"Well," George says, moving toward her again, "It's been such a nice evening with you here... I think I'm too excited to get to sleep."

"Sorry," Aimée says, edging down the lower berth and away from George. "I've disturbed you enough."

"Not at all," he assures her. "This is better than any dream I might be having."

Their eyes meet and another exchange of undeniable chemistry passes between them. "Besides," he continues, "what about this diary? You won't say just a little of what you wrote about me?"

Aimée looks down at her bare feet, wiggling her toes, distracted and nervous. "I shouldn't have told you, I'm sorry."

"Now that I know, there's no going back. It would only be cruel to hold out on me now." He winks at her. She darts him a glance, scowling sardonically.

"Don't give me that look," George says. "You just said you trusted me. So come on, just tell me one thing: What was your first impression of George Gershwin?"

"Stop it, George," Aimée says shyly. "I'm blushing."

"Blushing? Well then," George says, "it must have been quite a first impression."

"Well," Aimée says, wondering how much to reveal. "It was how you complimented my fingernails... but after you had been staring into my eyes." Aimée smiles, fondly remembering the moment. "I knew you wanted to say something about my eyes, but..."

"I thought it might seem untoward," George clarifies.

"That's what I thought it might be," Aimée says, snaking an arm around his waist and leaning in. "What do you say now, then? That the bridges have fallen between us?"

"I say..." George pauses for effect. "That your eyes are like two pools of sparkling emerald-green water, high up in the Catskill mountains. It was where I went camping a couple times as a kid.

There was this beautiful high-mountain spring, and your eyes are the colour of that crystalline water."

Aimée beams, her eyes sparkling with affection. "That's wonderful. You mean it?"

"Of course I do," George says, and they fall upon each other. He carefully, slowly slides off her belted nightgown and chemise, while Aimée fiddles with the buttons on his shirt, eventually ripping one of them off, sending it to the floor and into some dark corner, where it may never be found again. They kiss with patience and passion, the long night ahead of them to spare, and at last pull back the covers and crawl under the sheets. Along with the rhythm of the train, it's even better than the first time.

***

Early the next morning, Aimée sneaks out of George's cabin. Just as she shuts her door, the train slows down, chugging into what she can only assume is a small station on the outskirts of Berlin. She checks her wristwatch: Five o'clock in the morning. They still have two more hours until they reach Hauptbahnhof, the central train station in Berlin. The train slides to a halt as she burrows into her bunk. Just as she's ready to drift off, she hears a near-stampede of footsteps, as well as the garbled murmur of men's voices.

Despite her grogginess and fatigue, she can't help feeling like something is amiss. Why would so many passengers be boarding at what she knows must be a small station? *This is also supposed to be the express train,* Aimée thinks to herself, more than a little puzzled. Perhaps it *is* a busier station, and there's just some rowdy commuters going into the city for a day of work. But as she lays back on the pillow, she hears the voices growing louder, each new and distinct one speaking over the last.

The commotion is impossible to ignore, and Aimée gives up trying to sleep. Instead, she moves to the small mirror and begins to dress. First she rolls on a pair of cream-coloured stockings and matching brassiere. Then she dons a darted blouse in periwinkle velour, and a lavender, ankle-length skirt of cut velvet. She finishes the look with a skinny leather belt, fastened with a buffed-pewter buckle.

Peering out into the corridor, Aimée locks eyes with a gentleman of the Parisian police force. *Police?* she thinks to herself, then forces a pleasant smile, knowing that ducking her head back inside would appear suspicious. She opens the door and steps out into the hallway, still smiling politely.

An anxious-looking officer pushes forward from behind the others.

"Excuse me, Madame," he says to her in French. "But we've stopped the train as part of an investigation. We've got permission from the conductor to search the compartments."

Aimée, with nothing to hide, nevertheless grows a bit nervous at the mention of an investigation. But she nods and opens her cabin door for the policeman. "Of course," she says, ushering him in. "What sort of investigation?"

The policeman ignores her, scanning the room for a few seconds, then, takes down each piece of luggage and piles them up in the centre of the small cabin. Before Aimée can repeat the question, she hears George's voice in the corridor. "Oh well, go through whatever you need. I'm here if you have any questions." Then she steps back into the corridor.

Gershwin is in front of his cabin door, barefoot and still in a dressing gown, trying to communicate with one of the policemen in broken French.

"Parlez...?" he begins, then catches sight of Aimée. "Oh, Aimée, what on God's green earth is going on here?"

Aimée goes over to George and takes his arm. "There's an investigation," she tells him. "They have to search the cabins!"

"Oh my!" George says, clapping a hand to his mouth as one of the policemen takes his moment of surprise to push past him into the compartment. Aimée follows the officer inside and gets his attention. "Monsieur... you mustn't be confused. None of these belong to Mr Gershwin," she tells him in French. "They switched cabins. These are the personal effects of Maurice Ravel."

The officer turns to her with an expressionless look. He sports a waxed moustache below grey-blue eyes, clear and sharp as crystal. "It's a matter of the utmost haste," he says. "We haven't got the time to explain, but suffice to say that if we do find what we're looking for, then we will make an assessment as to whom it belongs."

George looks confusedly at Aimée. She waves him off and tries again to speak to the officer, who is throwing open cabinets and drawers. He then takes down the luggage like the other man did in her own compartment. "But," she says, "if you could just tell us what you're looking for, then we might be able to help."

The policeman mutters something in French, takes down the last of the suitcases, then addresses them both in English. "I'm detective Barthes. I'm in charge of the investigation, and all you need to know is that we must search every cabin on the train. It's something of a – How do the American's call it?" He turns to George. "…A formality. Now if you please, the best thing you can do right now is to wait in the corridor until we're finished. Then, we might have some questions… or we might not."

Aimée and George exchange a glance, then head into the corridor to wait. Ravel is out of his room as well, making a fuss and complaining of his dire need for sleep before a performance. He's wearing a sleeping cap, dangling comically over his tousled hair. Porters appear at the end of the hall, apparently to aid in the investigation. They knock on each cabin, asking the passengers to kindly step into the adjacent dining car while their luggage is searched. Gershwin turns to Ravel, just as the three of them are shown into the dining car, and the corridor is blocked by one of the porters wearing an apologetic look on his face.

The dining car is lined with brocade drapery, and the seats are upholstered in fine red velvet. George, Aimée and Ravel sit down at one of the booths. Dim sunlight is just now cresting over the horizon. Ravel looks bleary-eyed and more confused than both of them.

"I tried my best to keep them out, but they were so pushy!" Ravel declares, crossing his arms like a spoiled child. With a histrionic look of terror, he clutches at George's hands across the table.

"But you didn't let them into my cabin, did you George?" he asks in a trembling voice.

"I'm sorry, Maurice," George says. "There was nothing I could do to stop them."

Aimée attempts to defuse the situation. "I'm sure it will all blow over in a few minutes. There has to have been some mistake."

Ravel turns to Aimée with watery, bloodshot eyes. "Foutaise! Coming in full force like that? There must be something seriously wrong. Might there be a terrorist onboard?"

George pats Ravel's hand, at last able to extract his own from the French master's frantic grip. "I'm sure it's nothing of the sort. Let's just wait and see."

Ravel's face changes like a storm system in hyper speed, the myriad emotions clouding his judgement until he finally leaps to his feet with a shout of protest. "Wait just a minute!"

Ravel approaches the porter, leaning around his shoulders for a closer look down the corridor. "Now you listen to me. I'm heading to Berlin for a very important performance. My composition is being played, and I won't have my notes thrown out of order by a pack of half-witted billy-clubbers!"

The porter is too shocked to speak, but manages to keep Ravel from moving past him.

"Do you see that?" Ravel shouts. "They're taking all the luggage out into the hall! What's the meaning of that? This is preposterous. Why can't I offer up my own luggage for inspection? Why can't I oversee what's happening down there?"

"Just calm down, Monsieur," the porter says in French. "There's nothing to be concerned about." He looks into the corridor, where the officers are running an inspection assembly line, opening each suitcase in turn.

The porter turns back to Ravel. "The luggage will be safely returned to each compartment when the officers are finished. It won't be long now."

"But, but—" Ravel says, clearly having trouble holding himself together.

A man wearing a soot-streaked engineer's uniform appears at the other end of the dining car. "Not to worry," he calls out to Ravel, who spins round looking all the more panicked.

"Not to worry, you say? When all my most valuable compositions are being thrown into disarray for no apparent reason."

"There's a very good reason for it," the engineer says in French. "It's a safety concern, and until the Parisian police force is finished, there's no possible way we can continue to Berlin. In fact, if it goes on much longer, we may have to off-board everyone."

"But," Ravel protests. "We cannot fall behind

on our travel arrangements!"

Suddenly, detective Barthes appears at the threshold. Ravel spins round on him, pushing past the porter, who goes to stand beside the engineer. Aimée and George watch from the booth as Ravel leans in so close to the detective that their noses almost touch.

"Do you know who you're dealing with, Monsieur?" Ravel asks.

"Do tell," says Barthes. "Who am I dealing with, that's so important as to hold up my investigation?"

"Maurice Ravel," Ravel says, stepping back and inflating his chest. There's a brief, weighty silence while Ravel waits for the detective to praise him.

"If I'm supposed to know the name, I must say I'm not familiar…" says the detective.

"I…" Ravel stammers, completely baffled as to how a Parisian policeman could not have heard of him. He is one of the most famous pianists of the era.

George gets up and cuts in. "Gentleman, I'm sorry for the misunderstanding…" He extends his hand. "George Gershwin."

The detective shakes it quickly, then seems to

recall something.

"Feel free to take down our names," George says. "Whatever we can do to help."

"Hmm…" the detective says. "Gershwin… now that's a name I've heard before. *New York* George Gershwin?"

Ravel leers with jealousy at George.

"Uh, sure," George says, trying for modesty. "We just would prefer to get going again to Berlin as soon as possible. Like Monsieur Ravel said, there's a performance we must get to. Must start preparing in advance…"

"I understand completely, Mr Gershwin," the detective says, then looks back down the corridor behind him. "We were almost done. And look at that. C'est fini." The officers have just moved on to the next carriage, leaving the hallway clear of luggage again. "Come along then, I apologise for the inconvenience. But you should've said your name a bit earlier!" He winks at George. "We could've ruled you out."

Ravel pushes past the detective and George, rushing into his original compartment. Soon enough, his gripes and groans begin to filter through the walls.

The officer rolls his eyes and turns to George. "He is with you, right?"

"Yes, sir," George says with a calm smile. "We're a travelling pair of composers."

"Well," says detective Barthes, his voice down to a whisper. "I'm sorry for the trouble, but just between you and me, we were looking for an explosive."

George and Aimée share a look of surprise.

"But not to worry," the detective declares. "Most of the time, the tips we get are just paranoid people with too much time on their hands for senseless worrying."

"Well," Aimée says. "It's good to know we're safe."

"You can never be too careful," George agrees.

Detective Barthes doffs his cap and gives a little bow. "Thank you for your patience and understanding." He winks at George again. "It's not every day you get to meet an American celebrity."

Before George can answer, Barthes turns on his heel and makes for the next carriage. Aimée looks over at George with curiosity. "How do you like being recognised like that? Even overseas... It's impressive."

He turns to her with a humble half-smile. "Don't worry. It doesn't happen often enough to go to my head."

She returns his smile and busses his cheek with a kiss. "Try to get some sleep. I'll need you in high spirits tonight."

George laughs and tries to take up her hand, but Aimée blows him a kiss and edges out of reach.

"I'm serious," she says over her shoulder. "There's still over an hour until we reach Berlin. Go to sleep, Mr Gershwin." And with that, she disappears into her cabin, leaving George in the hallway with the ghost of her kiss on his cheek.

CHAPTER 8

After a rushed departure from the central station, Gershwin, Ravel and Aimée hail down a cab. Ravel rides up front with the driver, ignoring the cabbie's incessant attempts at conversation. It's clear to George and Aimée that Ravel is still fuming, so they hardly say a word on the way to the hotel. However, many a sultry glance passes between Aimée and George, as they practice romantic innuendos with their eyes. In the wake of Ravel's embarrassment on the train, a pall of silence follows them into the busy avenue, as the trio head for the double doors of the Carlsberg Hotel.

Once inside the lobby, George tries weakly at small talk. "Well, at least we had a nice cab ride. No searches and seizures in there."

"Fire him!" Ravel bleats, whirling on Aimée. His overtired voice makes an echo in the lobby, and several people turn toward the ruckus.

"Maurice," Aimée says through her teeth. "What are you talking about?" She smiles around at the other hotel patrons, making it seem like nothing is wrong. The lobby is wide and spacious, with a grand staircase and a mezzanine supported by four Grecian columns. The austere columns have acanthus carvings on their capitals, and white-marble plinths that could outweigh an elephant. Despite the frequent outbursts from his mentor, George is happily in awe of his European surroundings.

Ravel steps toward Aimée with a look of intense distress. Thankfully, he lowers his voice. "The pianist we hired is a bumbling fool. Fire him. Immediately."

"The pianist… Why?" Aimée asks.

"I'm doing it myself!" Ravel blusters, back at top volume again.

"Just a minute, Maurice," Aimée says. "He's so highly regarded!"

"So am I!" Ravel growls with impatience. "But I won't stop until *every* bumbling commoner knows my name."

George stands awkwardly off to the side,

smiling tight-lipped at the pedantic German onlookers.

"Lower your voice, Maurice," Aimée hisses. "I understand why you're upset. But we're selling tickets with his name on the bill."

"And playing a piece by Maurice Ravel!" he continues to rant. "The setup was wrong to begin with. But, we can save it now. Can you imagine the audience when they learn that the *understudy* has been replaced by the actual composer? They'd... They'd..." Ravel's face is beet-red with mania.

"Huh," George says, playing along. "I can see it."

Ravel darts his eyes at George, who is waving off one of the hotel staff. When George turns back to Ravel, he finishes. "You can play it, Maurice. Nobody knows the piece better than you." George looks swiftly at Aimée, as if to say, 'I've got this'.

"Of course I can play it," Ravel says. He finally seems to be cooling off. "But you're missing the point, George. People come to see a great artist's performance. I am that artist, not some fancy-fingered page-turner. The audience wants, and deserves, someone inspired, someone with their own sense of the music, with style, with confidence…" Ravel begins to trail off.

George picks up on the same train of thought. "Exactly. The composer playing his own piece, surely that's a commodity."

"Alas," Ravel says, placing the back of his hand on his forehead in all seriousness. "I'm no commodity, George… but you are!"

Aimée glares at George and crosses her arms. "You're both crazy."

"Hold on, Maurice," George says. "What happened to you playing it?"

"It's too cheap. Wouldn't fit. This way we add value, and both of us gain some decent exposure. Come now, I'm sure you didn't expect to be performing in Europe on your little vacation? How exciting!"

George sighs. "I don't know, Maurice…"

Aimée tries to cut in, but Ravel talks over her. "You could salvage the whole thing! Mr George Gershwin from the greatest city in America premieres my new work! Can't you just see it? Think of your name on the marquis, George."

"Sure, I can see it," George admits with genuine

interest. "But I can't play it."

"Can't play it?" Ravel's face is painted with shock and disbelief. "But I'll help you along with all the rehearsal you need! Don't you want to be great? Those luggage-gougers knew your pomp… Imagine what they'll think when you play something truly spectacular!"

George finally sees through Ravel's intentions. Instead of a masterful collaboration, Ravel would like to see George look like an incompetent pianist in comparison to the immaculate composition which Ravel has created. Thereby solidifying Ravel's reputation as a real artist, and the red-blooded Yankee as a floundering moron. And yet, George has a feeling he can make the performance his own, enough to set him apart from the music itself. And the grand, European stage may not present itself for a long time.

"I'm not going out on stage looking like an amateur asshole, Maurice," George grunts. "If this is going to happen, I've got to know what I'm doing."

Ravel drapes an arm around him and leads him along to the reception desk. "I'll be there with you, every step of the way. We've got a full three days to prepare."

Aimée let her breath out, too exhausted to say more. She gathers her baggage and follows the odd couple along to the mahogany-lintelled reception desk. They pick up their room keys and settle in for the night.

***

Three days later, the night of the performance arrives. The trio head to the concert hall with extra time to rehearse. Everyone's excited and a little overwrought. But Aimée looks the calmest, as her reputation is not at stake.

Ravel and Gershwin run off to a private rehearsal room to practice a little more, and Aimée goes down to watch the orchestra tune up. A gentleman in a fine tuxedo approaches Aimée, patting his bedewed forehead with a neatly folded kerchief. He's in his late fifties, with a hairline that ran for the hills, and thin white vestiges of curls over his ears. He sports gold cufflinks and a lace-frilled pocket square. "Where is Monsieur Ravel?"

He asks Aimée.

Aimée hasn't seen him coming. "Oh!" She turns to him surprised. "I'm sorry, Sir, just watching the orchestra tuning, it's all so exciting. I didn't see you coming. You must be Herr Heinemann," she replies, smiling sweetly. "Maur... I mean, Ravel... He's with Gershwin."

"Whatever for?" Heinemann asks. "He should be meeting with the orchestra!"

"He's teaching Gershwin the piano pieces," Aimée says matter-of-factly.

"What?" Heinemann cries in disbelief. "He doesn't know them already?"

Aimée shrugs. "I'm sure they've almost got it." She takes Heinemann's arm. "Now look at these wonderful musicians you've assembled. That should take your mind off Ravel."

Heinemann can't help but be charmed by Aimée. "Yes, well... I suppose you can't rush a genius like Ravel."

"That's exactly right," Aimée says, leading him closer to the orchestra pit. "Now just relax, and enjoy this moment of calm preparation. Your reputation precedes you, Herr Heinemann.

Running this theatre as well as you do. I can see the wheels have already been set in motion. Now's the time got to let go and let the show take shape as its own living thing."

Heinemann relaxes with Aimée on his arm. Nevertheless, the pre-show jitters are unrelenting. He smiles at Aimée and watches the orchestra, but he can't shake the nagging fear of Ravel and the New Yorker making fools of themselves. The theatre has seen better days, and they can't afford middling reviews so early in the season.

***

An hour later, Gershwin and Ravel are still holed up in the rehearsal room. Tonight, they premiere Ravel's Concerto in G Major, with a playing time of a little over twenty minutes. Gershwin struggles through the second movement, while Ravel paces, raking his hands through his silver hair.

"Do you need the commode, George? Slow down," Ravel pleads. "Or else go and come back so you can play it in the tempo I wrote it in! Go again – from the top."

"I'm playing it the best I can," George says, frustrated.

"You must be able to do better than that!" Ravel blurts. "I had to spend all night re-working those asinine line changes you made. All wrong! What's there now is exactly right. Just play that! I swear... sometimes I wonder if you can even read music."

George bites his lip, but just then Herr Heinemann knocks at the door, and Ravel goes to open it a crack. "Monsieur Ravel, ah, there you are! You're wanted on stage to begin conducting. Unless you wish some other celebrity to replace you? I hear Charlie Chaplin is in Berlin?"

Ravel forces a laugh and starts wringing his hands. "That's very funny, Herr Heinemann. Very funny, indeed." Ravel checks his pocket watch. "But it would seem I still have about fifteen more minutes to rehearse with my pianist before I need to join the orchestra in the pit."

Heinemann smiles cordially. "Yes, I would not want to disturb your process, Monsieur Ravel. But you see, in the theatre business, fifteen minutes early is considered on time."

No longer burdened by Ravel's hawkish

commands, George starts to break away from Ravel's second movement, and begins walking through his own Concerto in F Major.

As Ravel tries to buy himself a little more time, Herr Heinemann hears the change in music and pushes open the door, where he spies Gershwin, playing his own work. "My goodness," Heinemann gasps. "What is that he's playing now?"

"Out!" Ravel yells at Heinemann, angry at George for stealing the show yet again.

"But Monsieur…" Heinemann pleads, "One from you and one from our guest, Mr Gershwin?"

"No, no, no," Ravel fumes. "Nothing can be done last-minute! I'm the conductor, and I'll be ready in fifteen minutes, with the music we decided on." Ravel pushes Heinemann out and shuts the door. George, unaware of Heinemann's rant, returns to where he left off in Ravel's Concerto, and plays through the last of it perfectly.

George spins round on the piano stool and beams. "I think I got it that time!"

"If that's the case," Ravel says through a gritted smile, "Then play it again!"

Gershwin sighs and starts again at the first movement.

***

After only a ten minute-delay, during which the audience squirms in suspense, Ravel finally takes the stage, greeted by a round of rollicking applause. Opening night, and the auditorium is packed to the gills. A full house.

Gershwin makes it through the first two movements without any issues. When he reaches the third movement, however, the notes begin to bleed together on the page, and he begins to play the piece from memory and pure feeling. George Gershwin isn't used to reading music, but he hasn't yet divulged this fact to Ravel. And it's too late to switch back to the books so late in the performance. With a nervous shiver, he lets the lines on the page blur, and moves into the third movement, only a measure early.

Presto! Gershwin is hammering his way into the third movement at blazing speed, adding his own reckless, yet wonderfully original flair.

Ravel notices the difference. Gershwin's fingers noodle up and down the ivories, while Ravel's conducting grows ever more jerky, trying to take hold of Gershwin's attention, even thwacking the baton on the music stand, in an attempt to remind George to read the notes directly, and not to offer up his own interpretation.

George, as affable as ever, looks to Ravel with eagerness. He gives him a small, flourishing shrug. Ravel glowers at him and continues to jerk the baton with such stiffness that a deeper disparity grows between the written arrangement and the sounds coming from the piano. Yet the orchestra follows along, taking Gershwin's lead, staying within key as he broadens the scope of the composition.

The audience edge toward the front of their seats. The tirade of dissonance is nearing a breath-taking climax. George Gershwin is converting the performance into a showcase of his own virtuosity. The audience takes a collective breath of sheer excitement as they soak up this display of youthful exuberance. Gershwin is showing everyone just how perfectly he can breathe new life into a traditional movement, all by way of his knack for improvisation.

When the movement reaches its end, every member of the audience erupts in a fervent ovation. Save for the old and disabled, nearly everyone leaps to their feet, and the concert hall swells with praise for the one-of-a-kind performance. The ovation grows louder and louder, reaching its climax as George takes a bow.

George has never felt such elation before, yet, scanning the crowd, there's one face he wants to see most of all. Finally, he spies Aimée, high up in a balcony box on the right side of the theatre. She's jumping and clapping her satin-gloved hands together. George blows her a kiss, then waves to the rest of the crowd and bows again.

Gershwin then sweeps his hand toward Ravel, who has just climbed out of the orchestra pit. There's a noticeable dip in volume when Ravel takes his bow, and his face goes pink with chagrin. Perhaps the audience has grown tired of clapping so heartily for so long, or else Gershwin has stolen Ravel's thunder once again. Maurice Ravel thinks the latter, but he holds himself together and smiles politely, heading offstage just before Gershwin, waving to the crowd as he disappears from view, stepping into the shadowy backstage curtains.

***

Gershwin heads offstage as well, where he shakes hands with each of the orchestra musicians. Catching no sight of Ravel, he assumes it's his usual practice to vanish right after a show's conclusion. He figures it's one of Ravel's odd social habits. George heads up to the auditorium box where he saw Aimée. She's still there, sipping a 22 Riesling, and when she sees him her face lights up.

George kisses her quickly and discreetly. Their relationship is still under wraps. They chat for a minute or two, but soon, Herr Heinemann arrives offering to arrange a late dinner.

"Should the two of you be so inclined?" Heinemann asks.

"Two of us?" George asks. "What about Ravel?"

Heinemann tells them he's already supped and turned in. So Aimée and George order potato pancakes, beef roulade and a second bottle of Riesling.

"He seemed happy, didn't he? They all loved it!" George says, between bites of pancake.

"Part of it, yeah," Aimée says.

George gives a laugh, hoping she was kidding. "By that you mean… all of it?"

Aimée puts down her fork with a sigh. "The crowd… they loved the performance. And they especially loved how you played it, which Ravel *didn't* like. You gave the piece that something else it needed at the end. That panache…" Aimée giggles. "I watched some of the old ladies who had fallen asleep wake up when it happened."

"So that's great!" George says, beaming.

Aimée takes his hand, sensing an outburst if she doesn't explain properly. "I agree with you. It was the best performance I've ever seen, and I'm not one for concertos. I haven't even seen that many, but that's not the point." She fixes him with a serious look. Here's what happened – Ravel's intention was to make you look bad, and instead; the way you played *his* music made *you* look like a complete star. He may have thought you were showing off…"

"But I played his piece – just like he wanted! I

147

wasn't showing off. I'm the pupil to the master," George clarifies.

"Right," Aimée says, not sure what to believe, and too tired and full of roulade to care anymore. "I'm sure he'll sleep it off and feel better tomorrow. And if not, you can talk to him."

"Why should I have to talk to him?" George protests. "He's the one who asked me to play for him. He should be here with us right now! I didn't want to play the piece in the first place. I came here to have instruction in composition, not performance lessons."

Aimée chews a tender slice of beef and looks surprised. "Did he agree to that?"

George bites into a dinner roll and nods. "This afternoon. He promised me composition lessons. I think he was really excited about the show, and wanted to puff me up."

Aimée sighs, looking at George with affection that borders on pity. "George, if you haven't figured it out by now, Ravel can be quite unpredictable."

"I know, I know," George agrees. "But I can still hope. I've come this far, haven't I?"

Aimée swirls her glass of wine. "You've come

and gone very far, Mr Gershwin. It's true, but what have you learned from this weekend?"

George looks out from the auditorium box, and down to the empty, dimly-lit stage. "I've learned that I've got a lot to learn about music…" he turns back to Aimée, "and people."

"People are far more complex than music," Aimée says. "You can't play people."

George laughs, tips her a wink and takes another bite. Aimée blushes, happy to have impressed him, even a little.

After they finish dinner, they share a cab back to the Carlsberg Hotel, and retire to their separate rooms. Still no sign of Maurice. George lies awake for the agreed-upon half hour, thinking over the events of the day, and even though he worries about Maurice, his pride at having played his first European show is more powerful. As soon as the clock strikes eleven, he heads into the hallway and down to Aimée's room, where she lets him in, and they spend yet another night of passion together.

***

A week after the premiere, Ira Gershwin is sitting in a dingy Berlin hotel room. He's booked a stay in the Mitte district, far from the gilded palatial excess of Ravel's accommodations at the Carlsberg Hotel. Ira is not in town for sightseeing. He's heard news of the premiere in the Paris newspapers, and travelled to Berlin to surprise George at the next show. Ira is somewhat irked at having been left behind in Paris, but happy to hear that George is getting to play shows under the watchful eye of his esteemed mentor. Moreover, Ira is excited for the enhanced notoriety this European run of shows will bring the Gershwin name.

Inspired by his brother's exploits, Ira is hunkered down at his own creation. He huddles over a table and scratches away at a messy stack of parchment. The lines are so incongruous and the ink so badly smudged, that only a Gershwin brother could ever make sense of it.

A loud bang issues from the hallway. Unwilling to break his focus, Ira hopes it was only a radiator pipe. But another, louder bang comes next, and Ira straightens up to his feet. It was a knock at his door. He almost goes to answer it but, just in case, he scurries to fold his stack of papers away. At the top of the first page is the title of his next Broadway show, *Porgy and Bess*. He stows them carefully in the file folder which he tucks under a newspaper, then shuffles to the door, just as another knock rattles the door on its hinges.

"Hold on!" Ira says, fiddling with the lock.

The moment he turns the knob Wally Roberts bursts in.

Ira stumbles back while the big man barrels inside. "Wally? Why are you—"

Wally holds up a beefy hand. Ira falls silent. "Don't start with the questions. I'm the one who should be asking you assholes why the hell—" He stops mid-sentence, seeing only a single bed and no sight of the other Gershwin. "Well," Wally continues, "there's only one asshole here. But anyway, I can't believe you screwed me like this…" Wally surveys the stained carpet and peeling walls. "At least you're not spending *all* our money."

Ira shifts awkwardly on his feet, unsure of what to say.

Wally glares at him. "I can surmise why you're in Berlin: following George's time-wasting escapades, but what exactly are you doing, just sitting here in a trashy hotel room? Shouldn't you be tracking him down? We need to get George back to the States, and away from that buggering, bourgeois ruffian!"

Ira swallows. "I'm writing the next number… But Wally, look, I'm sorry you had to come all this way. Come and have a seat."

Wally laughs. "I'm afraid I'd break the furniture. Wouldn't want to run up the bill!"

"Oh c'mon," Ira says, taking a seat in a spindly, straight-backed chair. "It's not as bad as you think. And like you said, I'm saving money!"

Wally crosses his arms. "And what about your brother? Staying somewhere with the fancy, fraudulent, frog? Racking up room service tabs at the Carlsberg?"

Ira gives Wally a pained expression. "Well, I certainly hope he isn't staying there, and even if he is, I'm sure he isn't spending his own money. He must have an arrangement with Ravel…"

Wally's eyes pop out like a pair of peeled grapes. "You don't even know where your brother is staying?"

"Well," Ira says. "I know he's with Ravel. I was going to ask him after the show tonight."

"Well that much is obvious, Ira!" Wally shouts, fishing a folded newspaper from his pocket and fanning it out. Wally reads the headline with biting emphasis, *"Maurice Ravel Strikes Gold – American Flair for the Ears of Berlin."*

Ira opens his mouth to respond, but—

"This was supposed to be me!" Wally shouts, fuming. "You can see as well as I: He's playing you, Ira. What I still don't understand is why you're letting this happen! Do you like sitting around while everyone else around you are *striking gold?"*

Ira remains quiet. His only excuse would be to tell Wally more about *Porgy and Bess.* But Wally would never understand. Like George's time spent with Ravel, Porgy is a personal project, under the theatre-company radar. And besides, it's way too alternative for Wally's tastes – a man who would put on a single-chord reverie, if he was sure it would sell tickets.

Wally sighs and sits down on the bed. Ira's heart leaps, but luckily for him, Wally avoided the sheaf of 'Porgy' papers.

Seizing the moment of calm from Wally, Ira gets to his feet. "Come on, Wally. You're right. Let's get to the auditorium early. See if we can catch George before the show. Only thing for it."

Wally groans and starts rubbing his eyes. Then he glares at Ira with petulant dismay. After a quick, childish stare down, Wally gets to his feet and goes to the door. Without a word, Ira goes to the hook for his coat and hat, meeting Wally out in the hallway. Wally is still pouting, but Ira knows if he can keep the big producer moving instead of raving, he'll calm down by the time they get to the theatre. Ira has the concierge hail them a cab, and he heads out into the clouded afternoon with hopes for the best.

***

While Ira and Wally are on their way to the theatre to confront George, Ravel has him practising in the stuffy rehearsal room. As a light rain begins to pepper the window, the two composers start again on the Concerto in G. Even after five shows, Ravel is still unsatisfied with

George's performance. They're focusing on the third movement particularly. George forces the presto over and over, the fastest and most arduous part of the entire concerto. He's missing notes here and there, but has it by memory now, and playing quite close to how it is written. But it must be perfect for Ravel.

Sweat beading his brow, George plays on fiercely, determined to impress his mentor.

Alas, Ravel cuts him off. "Stop, stop, stop…"

Gershwin finishes the measure and sits back from the keys. "Ah… but it's close enough, Maurice! The audience loves us." George laces his fingers together to demonstrate. "You're helping me learn how to mesh, while I'm putting the American spin on things."

Ravel rolls his eyes. "I still can't believe how positive the reviews have been. You're butchering the third movement every time!"

"No matter, Maurice," George says with a grin. "I don't even remember what happens when I'm up there. I'm just *feeling* it out. Don't take it personally. I've never been much for reading music. But I promise, I am trying to play it correctly."

"I have a very hard time taking you at your word!" Ravel blusters.

Typical, George thinks to himself. *Unbending, unmoving Maurice Ravel.*

George makes an 'oh, pooh' gesture then tries to mollify the situation. "You have to admit, the applause has been wonderful, right? Every standing ovation is for you and me together... I just want to say again how grateful I am. To be onstage, playing at the level of my very own idol."

"Quiet," Ravel snaps, sitting down at the stool. "If we can't play it properly, then it's only empty praise. Now, allow me..."

Under the bench, Ravel's feet shuffle and kick George's aside from the pedals. "Here. Let's slow the tempo down to half-speed. Read along with me."

George obeys, trying to burn every note into his brain, and keep his impulse to improvise on a tight leash.

"My boy," Ravel goes on, playing his concerto in half-speed. "I'd like to apologise to you..."

"Really?" George asks, still following the notes on the composition sheet.

Ravel flips the page when he reaches the end. "Yes. I've conducted these past nights in poor taste. My heart has been filled with greed, and I pushed you to play because I wanted to control everything. In the end, although I manipulated you, nothing filled my heart in return. So, before the next show, I only ask that you play the concerto a single time in half-speed, focused on committing every note down to memory. As you've said, this is your preferred method. But you won't need me for that, so in the meantime, allow me to show you something new."

George perks up with interest, straightening his back into proper posture. Ravel starts the lead-in to 'La Valse'. The notes are dark and somewhat menacing, drifting in the minor key like St. Elmo's mirage on a stormy ocean landscape. George is surprised to hear something so psychologically motivated from Ravel. It only makes him all the more enamoured with his mentor.

Ravel steals a glance at Gershwin, and his lips curl into a small smile. "This is the piece I was commissioned to write." As he explains, the darker introduction blossoms into a bright sunrise bouquet, as if the pall of clouds on the horizon had simply broken with the advent of morning. "The melody takes its time," Ravel says. "It isn't marred by competing forces. It just sits and grows and grows."

George smiles, listening politely. He shuts his eyes to imagine the music, watching the sun break over the coastline in his mind's eye. He couldn't be happier in this moment, seemingly separate from all the bickering he and Ravel subject themselves to. *I'm still in his good graces,* George thinks to himself.

Ravel takes note of Gershwin's smile, swelling with the pride he subsists upon. "You get it, don't you? This, my boy, will be a return to form for me. Not every commission has to be so drab and dull. When you reach my level of popular appeal, you needn't simply follow the ho-hum of the mainstream." He reaches an ominous passage, where the bass chords seem to be churning up a storm again, and George imagines heavy clouds rolling to cover the sun once again. He opens his eyes, and Ravel gradually slows the piece down, then comes to a full stop.

"That's it?" George asks.

"Oh, heavens no! It goes on for a good while," Ravel declares.

"It's wonderful, Maurice," George says sincerely. "Thank you for sharing it with me."

Ravel gives an almost imperceptible nod, and seems to be fixing his face so as not to let his understudy see him smile. "I just wanted to apologise if I made you uncomfortable. The last few efforts with my concerto…"

"Oh," George waves him off. "It's nothing to worry about. The audience had a great time, that's all that matters. I can only play the instrument; I can't play the people." George laughs unexpectedly, thinking of how Aimée said it better. "I know what you mean now… An artistic success can also be critically acclaimed!"

Ravel's face flushes with colour. "Mon Dieú, you're completely missing the point!" He stands up, flailing his arms. "I can't pretend I like you! That first night… you stole my performance. You butchered and chopped and reordered the entire third movement! That was my piece… You were off! And you never even apologised. Were you not even aware of the artistic atrocity you committed?"

George gets up from the piano stool, gulping like a fish out of water. He was just settling in with the tender Ravel, and now the old master is all teeth and claws again. "I *was* following the music," George says in his own defence.

"You were so far off," Ravel shouts, "I can't see how you couldn't have been trying to go against me! The strings and winds were following right along… but where were you? Off in the weeds with that filthy improvisation. Changing the arrangement as you pleased!"

"I was right along with you," George says, starting to feel less sure of his assertions. Did he follow the piece properly? Now he couldn't be sure.

"No, Mr Gershwin. I wrote the piece and I would know. You melded it into some form of disgusting, congealed *jazz*." This last word rolls off his tongue like something infectious he wants to spit out.

"What about the shows this week?" George asks.

"Marginal improvement," Ravel says, pulling

his goatee and beginning to pace. "But the point is that you never apologised for the first performance, George. Imagine you were premiering a piece, like birthing a child, and the doctor delivers it with a severe deformity? Then acts like nothing is wrong, accepting all the praise for a healthy new-born?" Ravel pulls at the tufts of silver hair on the sides of his head. "Do I have to make up a story for you to understand? Is that some sort of thick-headed American idiosyncrasy?"

"I'm sorry, Maurice," George says, hanging his head. "I thought you were happy with it, because the audience approved. I should've known better."

Ravel barely hears the apology, muttering to himself, "If only I had been in better shape, I could've just played the damn concerto myself…"

"Maurice," George tries again. "I'm truly sorry."

Ravel turns to him, less flustered now, but still speaking in sharp, severe tones. "You played my piece, you *premiered* my piece, but you didn't play the notes, you played me."

"I'm sorry," George says, thinking back to what Aimée had said about Ravel not being happy after the first show. "I should have apologised earlier. But I latched onto the public reception. And then, with the other shows, everything got swept up in the moment, preparing for the next performance... I figured to let the first one go, but I shouldn't have."

Ravel gets in George's face, teeth gritted and eyes bugging out. "Yes," he hisses. "This little European stint is not about you. This is not a chance for the Yankee to be *en vogue*. Take all your petty jazz and nonsense and shove it. You're too timid to bring it into the rehearsal room with me, so don't you dare bring it into the concert hall again. You think because up there on stage I can't simply cut you off and end the show early. Don't think I won't! I must protect my reputation. I will not be infected. I will not be Americanised."

Ravel's face is as purple as George has ever seen it – a ripening eggplant. Spit flies from his lips, and George squints to avoid it. "You're the proverbial Locrian scale," Ravel blurts. "You're a flat second to me, George Gershwin! I'm the only composer here, you're simply the next generation... swayed by jazz demons. In fact, you're the devil itself...

You're the devil in music!"

George's jaw tightens. He's already apologised, and is sick of this lecture. "That's a lame insult, even for you," George says. "You've said your piece, and I respect your words, but if you continue to assail me with affronts, it's only going to stress me out! Don't you want me to play well tonight?"

Ravel grabs George by the collar. "People like you... why do they succeed?"

"Hey," George says, trying to pull away. "Maurice... Stop!"

"They liked Debussy," Ravel cries. "Now I have his slippers... Whenever I need to write something new, I always wear them... But, maybe I need to have them on more often. Maybe I'm losing my edge, but no... I can't become dependent." Ravel turns to Gershwin with a pleading look. All the anger has vented away, and only a hopeless kind of disquiet remains. "I've tried to do as Debussy would have," Ravel says. "So why don't they like me?"

"They like you, Maurice," George soothes. "What are you saying?"

Ravel clutches his head and makes for the piano

bench where he sits down again. "Ah... my head. It's all making my head hurt."

George sits down beside him, ready to pat him on the back, then thinks better of it.

"My head... So much talent, so much potential. And here I am with this reckless youth." He turns to look at George again, pinpoints of rage buried deep in his eyes, coming up to surface again in a fiery encore. "But your head... so capable, so bright and unclouded by age... And what does George Gershwin go and do? Garble it with *jazz!* Useless..." Ravel gets up again and crosses to the other side of the rehearsal room, where the mullioned window is now streaming with rain.

George rubs his own temples, all too fixated on his potentially garbled head. A wave of nausea comes over him. "Does it feel weird to you in here?" he asks Ravel, who's still turned away. "It's so stuffy..."

A moment passes as the men stand on opposite sides of the room. The tension settles a little as both of their tempers quell.

George's headache and nausea begin to subside, while the raindrops beat against the leaded windowpanes. Gershwin finally breaks the silence. "I'll go back to New York."

Ravel looks down at his feet, then quickly at George. "No. We should finish these performances. Only a few more to go."

"With all due respect," George says with a sigh, "I'm not sure how much I'm still getting out of this."

Ravel stares at the rain for a while, then turns back to George with a rueful stare. His eyes are red-rimmed, as if he's been crying. But it must be out of fatigue – George didn't see any tears. "I was getting the sense of that," Ravel intones. "It's because I'm not doing my part." He crosses back to the piano and sits beside Gershwin. "Do you want to know what makes us different from the rest of the world?" Ravel asks.

George nods, too nervous to steer the conversation.

"Come on then," Ravel says. "Let's try this again."

George waits a moment for the last of his headache to dissolve away. Leaning over the keys, he pretends it never happened, so he won't have to face the physical symptoms of his tumultuous relationship with Ravel. He glances quickly at the French master, then begins the concerto from the top of the third movement, always willing to forgive his volatile mentor.

CHAPTER 9

W
ally and Ira ride along in the taxicab. The silence is steady, and yet imbued with energy, like an empty church after a service. They arrive at the theatre where Heinemann has been putting on the performance of Ravel's Concerto. It's a seedy district, full of rep-houses and underground burlesque shows. Every other building seems to have been converted from an industrial warehouse, and more than half contain some sort of establishment serving alcohol and other vices. This is Weimar Berlin, where nearly every illicit narcotic substance is legal, and the winds of social experimentation blow freely.

Stepping out of the cab, a theatre with three floors looms over the two Americans. Wally hands the cabbie a handful of Reichsmarks through the window.

"You sure about this?" Wally frowns. "It's a bit small and dingy."

"At least it's taller than the other buildings…" Ira points out.

"Oh well," Wally shrugs. "What should I expect from a backwater country like this?"

Ira turns to the cabbie before he can drive away. He goes to the window and tries out his brutally slipshod German. "Ist das de concert theatre das musik?"

"Ja, Ja," the cab driver says with a simple nod, then pulls off from the kerb.

"Did you see how fast he drove off? Look at the state of this place," Wally complains. "First I had to fumble around in queer France, and when I couldn't find my *contracted* employees in Paris… where they were supposed to be, I had to head over to harum-scarum Berlin, where I'm stuck in some drug-addled tapestry of harassment!"

Ira turns to Wally, wincing a little. He knows that it's better to let him get it all out before they step inside.

Wally waves a sausage-like finger in the air. "I've been solicited by several street urchins, and that was only while I was wandering around, digging up your hotel address. Now you take me to *this* slovenly hideaway, where George is holed up with effeminate frogs!"

Wally spits on the street, then glares up at the rust-flecked theatre marquis. "I bet the police don't dare to patrol here. It looks like an effigy to the God of riots and looting! A palace for pickpockets! Sign úp to join the Thug's Brigade! Remind me again why you had to drag me along? Never mind, I remember. It's because your beloved brother is sniffing up some French freak's backside… diggin' for God knows what. Certainly not a paycheck!"

Ira takes out a pack of cigarettes, turning to Wally before lighting up. "Are you finished? Because I thought you wanted to get inside so we could have a word with the 'sniffer' himself…" Ira checks his wristwatch for effect, "before the show begins?"

"Right, right," Wally grumbles, leading the way up to the lobby doors.

Ira follows him closely, clapping a hand on his back. "Look, Wally. George *always* has a plan. This is a European theatre! I know it's not a Broadway marquis, but look at it like a gorgeous woman of a certain age, one who's too modest to know she's pretty." He winks at Wally. "Besides, it's the *inside* that counts."

"I have no idea what on earth you're talking about," Wally says. "I'm just worried about what's gotten *inside* your brother."

Ira scoffs, avoiding the insinuation. "Let's get going," he says. "The show might already have started." Wally, who was just getting ready to light a cigar, grumbles a bit, then follows Ira toward the front entrance.

Inside the lobby, only one of the ticket booths is un-shuttered. A clean-cut teller sits on a drafting stool, reading a skinny paperback. He looks up when the rowdy Americans enter the lobby, talking in rough voices and clearly disturbing the quiet peace within the lobby.

"Can I help you, gentleman?" the teller asks in near-perfect English.

Wally steps in front of Ira. "We're looking for George Gershwin. It's an urgent matter. You see, I had to come all the way over from New York to speak with him."

The teller regards him impassively. "I'm sorry to disappoint you, but Heir Gershwin won't be available until after the concert."

Ira sighs, fishing out his wallet. "So, it's already started. We'll have to buy tickets, then."

Wally's face becomes the colour of claret wine. "You don't seem to understand, mister. I've come a long way, and I represent Mr Gershwin. It's imperative that I speak with him immediately."

Ira leans in close to Wally and lowers his voice. "Do you really think this lackey is going to be able to go backstage and tell the director to stop the show? Don't be ridiculous. Once we buy the tickets, we can try and get backstage. You really must learn to pick your battles."

Wally opens his mouth – by reflex, almost always ready with some retort. But this time, he looks between the teller, who blinks nonchalantly, and Ira, who narrows his eyes. "Oh, fine then," Wally says, and pushes Ira aside. "Two tickets for the whole shebang. VIP if you've got it."

"I'm sorry, Sir," the teller shakes his head. "The box seats have been sold out, but seeing as 'The Threepenny Opera' is nearly over, I can give you a small discount."

Wally perks up, but then realises he's only

losing time with negotiations. "Just give us the tickets, buddy. I'm not pinching my pennies."

Tickets in hand, Wally leads the way through a set of velvet curtains. They walk down the central aisle, scanning the stage for George. It's cramped and smoky. To their surprise, it looks like the performance has already begun, but it's not George Gershwin and Maurice Ravel.

Wally grunts. "Is this what the great Maurice Ravel gets up to? There's only thirty people in here."

In fact, the house is at least three-quarters full, although at full capacity, the theatre couldn't hold more than two hundred people.

"This isn't Ravel…" Ira says, stroking his chin. "This must be that 'Penny Opera' he mentioned."

"Who?" Wally asks, and someone shushes him.

"The teller. The man who sold us tickets," Ira whispers.

"What could George possibly be getting from this? Talk about subordinate culture…"

"Well this is where George is," Ira says. "So, I trust he's getting something out of it. He doesn't give up when a chance lies before him."

"Right," Wally pretends to agree. "He's in here somewhere, wasting his time, your time, *and* mine. And instead of keeping track of him, you're sitting in your diapers in a dim-lit hotel room. What were you even doing in there?"

Ira refuses to rise to the bait. "Don't worry. This is just the opener. Some local guys, you know, a varied programme. Haven't you been to a concert before? Just listen!"

'Mack the Knife' is being beaten out heavily by a small jazz band.

"Is this some kind of queer theatre you've brought me to, Ira?" Wally asks. "Because that would really top things off!"

Ira cranes his neck around the theatre, trying to see into the shadowy backstage. He leans over an aisle seat and a young man clears his throat with impatience.

"Oh, sorry," Ira mutters. "Entschuldigung…"

"All this way," Wally whispers. "And he's nowhere to be found."

"George should be here," Ira says, growing a little worried. "Where is he?"

"Probably backstage, talking those pre-show

nerves with Ravel… The silver fox I'd wager they're both doing some buggering."

Finally, Ira has had enough. "Wally, really now. Are you trying to say my brother's a homosexual? Do you know how many women he has a week? He's here. If he is backstage, he's likely with a woman."

"On second thoughts," Wally scoffs. "You think they even have a backstage?"

"Wally…" Ira warns.

"What? Don't blame me!" Wally shouts, his volume indiscriminately high. "Blame your brother!"

Ira turns to leave, "Forget it, let's try and go find them anyway."

They hurry to the far-left side of the auditorium, where a set of stairs seems to lead up to the backstage. But the stairs are roped off, and just when Wally lifts the velvet rope to sneak in, a pair of ushers appear. They march down toward Wally and Ira, looking extremely affronted. They both cross their arms, blocking the stairs.

Ira throws up his hands. "Sorry… Sorry, Sirs."

"We were just a little turned around," Wally

says with a smarmy smile.

"Please," one of the ushers says. "Return to your seats, gentlemen. The main programme is just about to start…"

***

Ravel, Gershwin and the orchestra make their way through another performance of 'Concerto in G'. The first two movements play out like before, but Gershwin begins to take the lead towards the end. Ravel shoots daggers at Gershwin this time, whipping his baton with frenetic swipes, keeping the orchestra line with the written music.

Gershwin comes out of his improvised stupor, turning his eyes quickly to Ravel. Their eyes lock, and Ravel presses his lips into a thin line, then anchors the rest of the third movement with aplomb. George has no choice but to diminish his keystrokes, following the lead of Ravel and the orchestra. When the last, sonorous vibration of violin seeps into silence, the crowd erupts with another standing ovation. They still cheer loudest for George when he takes his bow, but Ravel knows the music was finally played properly, so he joins hands with Gershwin and raises both of their fists. The gesture is granted another warm round of applause.

Gershwin sees Aimée standing and clapping in the audience, nodding in acknowledgement that this was a far superior outcome. George also catches sight of Ira and Wally pushing their way down to the front of the stage.

Gershwin and Ravel take in the applause for a few moments more, then make their way backstage. Ravel shakes Gershwin's hand and gives him a small nod, then heads off to disappear as usual.

"Wait a minute, Maurice," George says. "Didn't it go especially well tonight?"

Ravel turns back. "Perhaps the best so far. And?"

"Well then, come on down to the front and have a little social hour with us. If you don't feel like talking to anyone from the audience, Aimée will be there too. She can keep you company."

"My boy," Ravel says, "I have no such thirst for the limelight as you… but as you performed to a satisfactory degree, I shall humour you this evening."

George will take what he can get from Ravel at this point. He beams, shakes Ravel's hand again, and they head off through the backstage hallway and into the auditorium.

George waves happily at the patrons collecting their things and heading out. "We'll be in the lobby for a while, come and have a cocktail!"

Some people look enthused, others are eager to get out of the theatre and return home. A crowd of about fifteen patrons ends up gathering with Ravel and Gershwin in the lobby. Heinemann brings over a salver of champagne, and the rest of the small theatre staff take simple drink orders. As George tries awkwardly to accept thanks in Germany, Aimée appears at their side, and soon enough starts to translate. A few more concert-goers flock to George's side, including Ira and Wally.

Wally pushes past a frail and balding gentleman with a cane and calls out, "Hey, refugee!"

"Arschloch Amerikaner… Scheisskopf," the man mutters.

Wally ignores him and steps up to George,

Aimée and Ravel. Ira follows timidly behind.

"Wally?" George asks, a little surprised. "I would've expected you, Ira. But Wally... all the way to Germany? What's the occasion? Came to see your most famous artisan spread the Gershwin name across the globe?"

Wally gives a big, patently false laugh, and the side conversations fall to a lull. "The occasion is getting you back to the States. We have a deadline, remember?"

George laughs it off, glancing about the room as if to quell the nervous energy of the onlookers. "Of course I remember," George assures him. "Who says I wasn't working on it this whole time? And look at this cohesion, Ira helped you find me right away!"

Wally steps forward with an oily smile, his frustration apparent even from outside the circle of conversation. "George... I didn't need, nor could I rely on Ira to keep me abreast of your cavorting. I read it in the Paris newspapers. Ira didn't tell me shit. So... if you're all done with this dog-and-pony show, let's head back to the city. Time's-a-wastin'."

Ravel sighs, loud enough for Wally to hear.

Wally spins to face him. "Whatsa' matter, old hat?"

Ravel leans over to George with a stage-whisper, his voice still loud enough that everyone close by can hear. "Does he *ever* shut his mouth?"

George guffaws, smiling widely at Wally. "Wally Roberts? No, not really… But that's his job, Maurice."

Wally rolls his eyes, refusing to look at Ravel. "Here's how it is, Georgie. Broadway is bleedin'. Ira's already got the lyrics goin', but we can't do nothin' without you. Everything's lined up for you to write the ditties."

George turns to his brother, surprised. "Ira? That so?"

"I…" Ira stalls, pale stricken. He was hoping he wouldn't have to chime in.

Wally claps Ira on the shoulder so hard that the Gershwin brothers both wince. "It's true," Wally says. "Ira's been writing every day since you ditched him in Paris." Wally winks at Ira. "That's right, I know you tried to not let me see it, but I saw that bundle of composition sheets under the bedspread. You can't fool the greatest music manager in New York City!"

"You could be the greatest in Berlin, too!" George cuts in, and everyone laughs, except Ravel. Even Aimée snickers a little.

"Haw, haw," Wally says. "Anyway, your brother's a madman like you. Doesn't stop working, and neither do I. So, this is me working – bringing you back." He wags a finger at the Gershwins. "You two geniuses should never be kept apart."

George and Ravel share a glance. George looks quickly at Aimée, then back to Wally. "Well, we can wrap things up here, I suppose. How about a few more days in Paris on the way back, hey, Wally?"

"That's a laugh, George." Wally narrows his eyes, fed up with the off-the-cuff negotiations. "We're catching a plane right out of Berlin. Tomorrow. No more excuses." Wally smiles around the small circle. "Deadlines haven't budged. I'm just ready for a long flight and an even longer bath. They say the air in Berlin… you know, it's a bit *soiled*."

"Wally…" Ira says.

"Relax Ira, I'm done now." Wally takes a glass of champagne from a passing usher. "Cheers to a good run. Not a bad show." Nobody returns his toast, but he gulps the glass down anyway. "See ya at the airport, Gershwins. Tomorrow, nine o'clock. I'll have your tickets."

"I should retire," Ravel yawns, watching Wally waddle away.

Ira looks to his brother. "Well, George, what now?"

George puts an arm around Aimée, who offers her hand out bashfully to Ira. "It was a pleasure to meet you, Mr Gershwin," she says.

"Sure, it was nice to meet you, too," Ira says, taking the hint. He says his goodbyes, shaking Ravel's hand and a few others from the circle of excited audience members. Finally, Ira tips his hat to George and steps away. "I better see you tomorrow, brother."

George waves him off, already heading outside to hail a cab with Aimée and Ravel. "No problem," George calls out. "Enjoy the last evening, brother. Lots to do in Berlin, but don't forget to sleep!"

***

Back at the Carlsberg Hotel, just past 11pm, George sneaks over to Aimée's room again. His heartbeat shudders in his chest as he waits for her to open the door. She's wearing a pearl-white chemise and black stockings, her black hair brushed into waves.

"Wow," George says, "Must be the last night in Berlin."

She passes him a glass of champagne. "But not the last with you."

"What makes you so sure?" He asks.

She presses a finger to his lips. "Just a good feeling. But let's pretend that it is our last night…"

Spilling champagne on the antique side table, George waltzes Aimée along past the kitchenette and over the luxury carpet, monogrammed with the Carlsberg logo. They kiss and pull at each other, diving in and out of each other's grasp. By the time they reach the four-poster bed, she's already got his belt loose and his trousers unbuttoned.

As George slides off Aimée's chemise, he tries to force thoughts of the day from his mind. But the stress of Wally's arrival still weighs on him. He pulls back from kissing her and holds Aimée by the shoulders, taking his time to follow the milk-white curve of her shoulder with his eyes. Soft shadows fall across her breasts. He kisses her slowly and tenderly, tracing a hand down to the small of her back.

They move slower after that, ebbing and flowing in the passion of the present moment, sliding out of the rest of their clothes and under the sheets. Berlinese streetlamps silhouette their twining bodies, looking like shapes cut out from a shadowbox.

George finds himself wishing that time would stand still. It hits him all at once – he's leaving tomorrow, and it will be a very long time before he sees Aimée again. The pressure to spend the last evening together in bliss... it's too much for him, and he begins to lose focus, wondering how he's going to feel the next day, and over the weeks to come. George knows he can't fight it when a thought gets fixed in his mind, so he tries to lower the temperature between the two of them. He kisses Aimée a bit lighter, widening the space between them just a little, then finally pulls away with a sigh.

"What's wrong?" Aimée asks.

"I'm sorry Aimée..." George almost tells her why he's distracted, how he's overcome with worry about missing her. He stares into her eyes for a moment, then sits up against the headboard. She snuggles up beside him, pulling the sheets to her neck. So as not to upset her, George decides to cover his tracks with another concern. "It's not you, Aimée. I want us to have a good last night together... But, when I go back to New York, do you think I'll ever get a piece of my own?"

"What do you mean?" she asks.

"My own performance..." George says candidly, realising that even though he's leaving out some of the truth, he doesn't have to lie to Aimée. Much of his mental strain is coming from the uncertainty awaiting his career. "I want my own concerto, where the people come to hear *my* music, not Maurice Ravel's. Not some other composer."

"I'm sure that will happen for you," Aimée assures him.

"But when?" George asks, not waiting for an answer. "I need her... She's the only one who will ask me to write something." His hands twist up in the bed sheets, beginning to tremble.

"Who?" Aimée asks, sitting up to better see his face.

"It's nothing like that," George says. "It's… Janus…" George winces in pain and rubs his forehead. He gets out of bed and shuts the blinds. "Jesus, don't they ever put those lights out?"

Aimée slides to the edge of the bed. "What's really the matter, George?"

George sits on the bed beside her, taking up her hand. "It's not about you, Aimée. The demands of my career will keep us separate, at least until I can get in good with Janus. She's a powerful patron, you see. Ravel has the Conservatoire… Well, Janus is my ticket to that world, where my music won't simply be Broadway drivel."

"All in due time, George," Aimée says, trying to pull him back to bed.

George gently lets go of her hand. "It's time, yes. But it's not that simple. I'm not really a free man, you see. Going back to New York is just the beginning. Ira and Wally want us to go to Hollywood to write for the movies."

"Doesn't that excite you?" Aimée asks.

George puts on a grim expression. "I don't think I'll make it in California."

"Okay," Aimee says, a bit coldly. "Then don't go."

"If I get to Hollywood, I just have this bad feeling," George says, "that my chance to make the sort of impression on music that I want to… is going to slip away. So I must impress Janus, before Ira gets up the gumption to move west."

"George, what are you talking about? Bad feelings?" Aimée asks, entirely puzzled, and a little bit jealous of the other woman.

George gets up from the bed, driving his fists into his temples and kneading the flesh. His head is throbbing, his heartbeat slow and feeble. "If only it were enough to be popular and well-liked… If only I hadn't seen all this. Playing those shows… The audience so finely dressed. An audience that really listens. People who care more for music than entertainment…" George trails off, muttering.

Aimée sighs, falling back on the feather pillows. "If you need to talk sensibly, I'm here. But you know better than to worry about something like this, especially at this hour. I'm going to sleep You should do the same, George. It'll be better in the morning." She curls up in the sheets and turns away.

Alone with his thoughts, George goes to sit at the window seat. His face is lost in shadow. *Last night in Europe,* he thinks to himself. No matter how he tries to sort out the situation, Janus seems to be the only answer. He isn't even excited to return to his cosy apartment in the East Village.

George is dreading everything about New York City, except for the slim chance of seeing Janus at the bar again. And what about Aimée? *Maybe someday I can come back,* he thinks. But knowing how fed up Wally was, he doubts the possibility. Maybe he could fly Aimée over to the States, but this option breaks down as well. Without control of his own career, he won't make a promise to Aimée that he can't keep. After an hour of pondering, the headache subsides, and George returns to his own room to sleep for a few hours.

CHAPTER 10

The following day, George, Ira, Wally, Aimée and Ravel head to the Berlin airport. While Wally picks up the tickets, George pulls Aimée aside for a quick moment to apologise for his mood the previous night. She tells him she understands and does not hold it against him. Wally returns with the tickets and everyone heads out to the tarmac together.

"Well, Maurice. Thanks again for everything," George says, shielding his eyes from the sun off the blacktop.

"The pleasure has been mine," Ravel says, his words a little hollow.

"Well, yes. Thanks, are in order. But we should really be going," Wally says.

George ignores him. "Maurice, you must come to New York the next time you want a healthy distraction."

Ravel nods politely, feigning interest in such an

idea.

George turns to Aimée and offers an embrace. "Aimée, goodbye…"

"Goodbye Mr Gershwin," Aimee replies, hugging him back.

"Thank you for taking such good care of us," George says.

"It was a great pleasure getting to know you," Aimée says, giving a small curtsy, then turns to shake hands with Ira. Wally is already heading for the plane, waving them along. Ira tosses a final wave and heads for the plane.

"Well," George says to Ravel and Aimée, "until next time."

"Adieu, Mr Gershwin," Ravel says, tipping his felt hat.

George turns to catch up with Wally and Ira.

"Well, did you screw her?" Ira asks, as soon as they're out of earshot.

"That's not how I'd put it," George says. "But if you must know…"

"Okay then," Wally cuts in rudely. "Then you've gotten what you came for, haven't you? Now let's fly the fuck home!"

Ira rolls his eyes and follows Wally. George takes one final glance toward the terminal before ducking into the rear door of the plane. His stomach is queasy all through take-off, but after a few whisky tonics, George finally relaxes, puts away his compositions, and goes to sleep.

***

When the Gershwins return to their Manhattan apartment, George leaves his luggage unpacked and heads straight for the baby grand piano along the wall of steel casement windows. After unpacking, Ira swings open some windows, letting the city's breath pervade the apartment. Ira looks over his own letters, then brings over George's much larger pile of mail, including everything from while he was abroad. Ira sets the bundle on top of the piano, but George barely flicks his eyes at the stack. Instead, he returns dutifully to a brand-new composition, *An American in Paris*.

The phone rings, and a few seconds later, Ira appears. "I've got Wally, here, George. He wants to *personally* remind you about the other half of the

Paris deal."

George waves him off, even as Wally continues to bark through the receiver.

George looks up from the keys with a pleading look. "Ira, it's a terrible time. I'm right in the middle of…" but George is in a corner and he knows it. It's obvious he isn't working on Wally's production.

"Okay, fine," George says to his brother. "I'll talk to him."

"Thank you," Ira says, silently mouthing the words, then passing George the receiver on the extension line.

Wally Roberts chortles away. George hems and haws, then after about a minute he passes the phone to Ira.

"Hello," Ira says into the receiver. "Wally?" But the line is dead.

"Everything's fine," George says. "Right to work on 'Oh Kay'. Twenty hit numbers and an overture."

Ira crosses his arms and clicks his tongue, but George has already turned back to working on the same composition as before.

"That's the same damn thing you were just

on," Ira protests.

"Wally's all cheery again," George insists. "What's the matter? I'm *working* on it."

Ira throws up his hands and walks away. He sets the receiver back on the phone with a loud snap, darting his eyes at his brother, who takes no notice.

"Working on it... right after this," George mutters, then hunches over the keys again. He noodles his way through another measure, then scratches in the notes with a fountain pen on the composition pages. His suitcases from Berlin sit along the side of the room with their buckles fastened. Untended and unpacked.

***

Later that evening, George heads to the Manhattan Nightclub, where he sits by the bar, scanning up and down for any sign of Janus. It's a lively time of night, and the room is filled with murmurs and intermittent laughter. An overflowing ashtray sits beside him. He puffs away, chain-smoking as usual when he's nervous and impatient. Next moment, a gregarious, portly fellow ambles up to George.

"Hello, there, young man," the chubby man says. "Word of your forays in Berlin have travelled far!"

"I spent more time in Paris, actually," George says in a weary voice.

"Ah, well," the man laughs, "someone like you must be going everywhere! Young and spry, you've got the gas for it."

"Yes, well, it was very... exhilarating," George says, not feeling young at all.

"Back in the city with big plans, huh?" the man asks. "Gonna bring that dulcet European fare to the Broadway stage?"

"They'd hate it," George says, taking a drag. "In fact, I'm pretty sure you'd hate it, too."

"I beg your pardon?" the man asks, his wobbly jowls quivering.

"Never mind." George looks past him, scanning the bar. "Have you seen a young woman hanging around here tonight? Real thin, dark hair... She's got a lot of..." he trails off, seeing many women here who fit the description. Peering through clouds of smoke, he squints his eyes at the lights and swirling, dancing faces. Head swimming, he clutches at his temples and rubs at his eyes.

"What then, my boy?" the man asks. "A lot of what?"

"A lot of… better things to do," George says. "Anyway, I should get back to writing."

"Oh, don't mind me," the man says with a look of mild concern. "Nice to meet you. Keep it up, kid!"

"Thanks," George replies. "I'll see ya."

Shaken by the sudden headache, George pushes back from the bar, leaving his drink unfinished. He slaps a few bills on the counter and heads for the door. Outside, he decides to walk home instead of a cab, hoping the fifteen blocks will clear his head.

***

Back at the Yorkville apartment, George heads straight for the piano. Ira isn't there. *Hopefully out drinking for a long while*, George thinks to himself, then spends an hour composing *An American in Paris*. Just as he gets up to make himself a drink, someone buzzes the doorbell.

George shrugs, hoping they will go away. Busying himself with a Tom Collins, the bell rings again. This time it startles him, and he nearly nicks his finger while cutting the lemon. George curses, then has an idea. Leaving the drink unfinished, he dashes to the piano, waiting for the buzzer to ring again.

This time the buzzer drones on for a full five seconds. Someone is out there, leaning on the button. George plays a few scales, finding the right key for the doorbell. To his delight, he finds the note in the G major scale, the same key signature as *An American in Paris*. The buzzer sounds again in three short bursts, and George incorporates the notes into the piece, full of ideas about instrumentation. He wonders aloud, "Could these staccato tones be played by actual car horns? Like the ones from the taxis in Paris? Would they allow something like that in the orchestra? Another form of percussion, you might say…"

The buzzing comes again in rapid-fire – too jarring to work with.

"Ugh…" George groans. "Get lost, huh?!"

Quiet for a moment… George hovers over the keys.

Bzzz! Another round of doorbell punches. George throws up his hands and dances over to the intercom. "What?" he screams into the speaker-box.

Kitty's voice crackles through. "George, it's me."

"Ah, Kitty," George says wearily. "It's a terrible time. I'm busy with the show. You know that. I'll see ya tomorrow."

"But it's *about* the show!" Kitty pleads.

George glances at the clock – just past eleven.

"An hour," he tells her. "I'm giving you an hour."

George presses the button to open the street door, unlocks the apartment door, then hurries back to the piano where he jots down the presto-staccato buzzer notes.

Kitty comes up and cracks open the door, knocking softly.

George mutters a greeting, "Hey, Kitty. Come on over and tell me what it is."

Kitty lopes over to the baby grand piano,

draping her hands over his shoulders. George switches over from *An American in Paris*, to the partially finished score for 'Oh Kay'.

"So," Kitty muses. "You really are working?"

"Of course I am," George says, fluttering the keys. He plays on and Kitty dawdles beside the piano, rubbing his shoulders until he shakes her off, then she fiddles with the hem of her flapper skirt. Anything to grab his attention.

"So," she finally says with a little sigh. "How was your trip?"

"Yeah, good, Kitty," George says. "But this can't be one of our evenings. Come now. What's this about?"

Kitty flips her hair and saunters in a half-circle behind the piano bench. "Just wanted to run through a few songs. That is, if you've finished them?"

"Sure, sure, I've got plenty of finished numbers," George says.

Switching key signatures without lifting his eyes, George rambles into 'Someone to Watch Over Me'. Reaching the first verse, Kitty lays a hand on the piano lid and starts to sing.

"Won't you tell him please to put on some speed... Follow my lead," she sings in a sultry voice. "Oh, how I need someone to…"

Kitty sings softly, lazily following the structure of the song, not at all how the Broadway performance should go, bringing her lips closer to George's ear with every bar.

When her hair finally brushes his cheek, he moves away. "Kitty. We only have an hour, remember?"

"I remember," Kitty purrs. "Sixty *long* minutes… But that's enough rehearsal."

Kitty reaches around to the back of his neck and pulls him into a kiss. George kisses her back and spins round on the bench. It wobbles on its feet and nearly topples over. George regains balance and kisses her neck. As Kitty moans, he unbuttons her skirt and it falls to the floor.

***

Two hours later, George and Kitty lay sprawled in his bed.

George lights a cigarette. In the dim light of the

cherry-glow, he notices a glint of metal on the night table. His wristwatch. Cursing under his breath, he fumbles to check the time. "Damn." He turns to Kitty's supine figure. Her eyes are half-shut and she seems completely relaxed. George whispers into her ear. "Kitty, I'm sorry... But you have to leave."

Kitty sits up on her elbow. "Got what you wanted then? Pardon you, asshole!"

"Kitty... Come now, I said I had an hour, it's been almost three. I really must finish the score for tomorrow. We have rehearsals, remember?"

Kitty lights her own cigarette, then gets out of bed. George gets up, reaching for his crumpled heap of clothes to get dressed again.

Kitty stands there stark naked, enjoying her cigarette.

George pauses in admiration, then resumes dressing. "Kitty—"

She cuts him off. "That's what I like about you, George, you're so driven. You always have time for your composition..." Kitty goes to the dresser and slips on her negligee. "But making time for people has benefits, too."

George starts to button up his shirt. "I appreciate the advice."

Kitty shakes her hips to slide into her skirt. "George Gershwin. Busy, musical genius… I just wish my advice wasn't *all* you appreciated. Maybe I'll find someone who appreciates *me*." Kitty smirks and pulls on her blouse.

George moves toward her. "I *did*… I *do* appreciate you, Kitty."

Kitty clicks her tongue and turns on her heel. "Oh George, it's so cute what you think you can get away with. I won't wait around for you forever."

George starts to stay something, but Kitty shuts the bedroom door and is gone.

***

Next morning, George strides into the rehearsal room with a puffed-up confidence and ever puffier circles under his eyes. Tucked in the crook of his arm is the finished score for 'Oh Kay'. While the orchestra tunes up, Ira and Wally look up from their cups of coffee.

George nods to both of them. "Gentlemen,

pleasure to see you."

"Oh good," Wally says, seeing the pages under George's arm. "Maestro, what've you got for us?"

"Oh, just my side of the deal," George smiles, "twenty hit numbers and an overture."

Ira beams. "What did I tell you? Don't underestimate a Gershwin brother. Gimme a look-see."

Wally takes hold of the pages before Ira can. "Gershwin the genius only has one copy. So – everyone take a break and we run-through in an hour. Joey, go and make some carbon copies, and bring me a croissan'wich, too!"

Joey, the runner, appears for a split second. Just long enough to snap up the new score. "Yes, Mr Roberts!" he shouts, then scurries off.

Ira rubs his hands together. "Okay, George. You got Wally fooled, but what's this? 'Treasure Girl' revamped?"

George frowns, heading for the piano. "I've been working on it flat out since we got back. You should know, you've been on my case every minute."

"Get outta here," Ira says. "We've been back a

week. Even if you worked through the night..."

George gives him an easy smile. "That's exactly what I've been doing."

Ira waves his hands. "At this rate, we can knock out a new show every week! If it's not a load a' bull, that is."

George shrugs, opening the piano lid and socketing the half-prop. "You'll see for yourself soon enough."

Ira smiles. "I'll save my congratulations for *after* the rehearsal."

George hits a few chords, setting up his hand positions. Ira goes off to find Wally. The rest of the room falls to a hush, readying in anticipation of the copies coming back.

***

Ninety minutes later, everything is set for rehearsal, and Wally is demanding a second croissan'wich. Joey darts out of the room again, while George sits at the ready with the score perched on the music desk. The cast is in plain clothes, awaiting directions onstage.

Ira appears at the edge of the stage. "Okay. Picking up right off with the new material. This is act two, scene four. And… action."

George's nostrils flare and he sniffs sharply. He plays out the intro and the dancers hit their first marks. Wally gives Ira a nod of approval as the ensemble make their way through 'Oh, Doctor Jesus'. However, Gershwin starts to meander away from the notes as written, throwing in arpeggios and tangential melodies. The cast look around with confusion, but still manage to stay on beat.

Ira rushes over to George, waving at the cast to take a pause. "Stop, stop, stop."

George blinks and stops playing.

Ira puts a hand on his brother's shoulder and leans in. "What the hell, George?" He speaks in a forceful whisper, but nobody else in the room can hear him. "Now's not the time for that, brother."

The room steals glances at George. They cannot fathom why Gershwin would break off into utter nonsense, as if banging the piano keys at random.

George snatches up his manuscript. "Oh, for fuck's sake. It's a rehearsal – we rehearse things." He glares hard at Ira and storms out.

Ira turns to the cast. "Jet lag is a... Oh well, let's take ten minutes. I'll go and see what's the matter."

George nearly reaches the end of the hallway when he hears a door bang behind him. Most likely Wally or Ira coming to cheer him up. But if anyone called out, George didn't hear it. His own thoughts are too loud, careening off the walls of his scattered mind. *One moment, I was playing the piece to perfection, and then... Snap! Everything a blur.*

George only knows that he lost control of his fingers, and whatever he'd played had upset the whole room. *And of course, they blame me... As if I could never make a mistake.* George takes the stairs and goes for a diner coffee. Luckily, whoever was following decided to leave him alone. The waitress takes one look at George, then offers to make him an Irish coffee instead. By his second cup, George starts to feel like himself again.

CHAPTER 11

A few weeks later, Ravel hobbles into the chateau kitchen with a fruit basket. Aimée looks up from checking the mail, watching him shuffle to the table and open the basket lid, humming to himself all the while. She lets him have a moment before clearing her throat.

"Maurice," she says, "there's a letter here from America."

Ravel pretends he hasn't heard anything. He preens and poses around the room, trying to hide the soreness in his legs. He looks like a hyperactive child with an ankle sprain.

"Aimée, I've had the most invigorating ride from town. I'm too inspired to read any mail. I must start work immediately."

Aimée first looks at the rusty bike on the rack, then back at Ravel, wondering what he meant by 'ride'. She sighs, considering the money he must've spent on the taxi, when finances are getting scarce.

"Just take these vegetables I've procured," Ravel goes on. "Have them prepared so Marianne can make us a hearty ratatouille. I must get to the piano at once."

Despite his apparent urgency, Ravel seems to be waiting for something. Aimée peers into the basket and gasps. "What have you done?" She pulls out a carrot. "What can Marianne do with a single carrot?" She pulls out a single radish and a puny onion. "Whatever possessed you to only buy one of everything?"

"Variety," Ravel says, as if he coined the phrase himself, "is the spice of life. Marianne only ever gets the same combination…"

Aimée sighs. "You hate crowds, you're just trying to make a point. You keep on threatening to let Marianne go, but you won't admit you need her around." Aimée purses her lips, while Ravel starts to untie his shoes, ignoring her.

"Anyway," Aimée continues, "This letter is from George Gershwin, requesting formal lessons in composition. He says you're the perfect tutor, and he's allowing you to name your price."

"Mon Dieú," Ravel says, heading for the door. "I cannot oblige the frivolous jazz prodigy. Be sure to say no, but ask Mr Gershwin if he happened to acquire any of my luggage pieces after the mix-up on the train to Berlin. You remember how I'm missing my leather trunk? I'm thinking it may have walked off with Gershwin."

Aimée ignores the matter of missing luggage. "It would be best if we didn't waste money," Aimée says. "I'm sure George Gershwin can pay handsomely. What's a few extra hours a week? You already know you get along well with him."

Ravel gives Aimée a look of death. "Really?"

Aimée is bound and determined. "Maurice. It's a big cheque. Marianne, the chateau, having every vegetable." She waggles the carrot toward him. "Everything has cost."

Ravel shakes his head. "For once you are correct, because right now, *you* are the one costing too much! I see another letter there, one with a French postmark. Give me that one if you must distract me." Aimée narrows her eyes and hands over the letter.

"Thank you!" Ravel says, whirling away to his piano.

***

A few days later, Ravel sits at a long wooden table. Across from him is the long-faced principal of the Conservatoire, as well as a senior professor with shaggy eyebrows, and two grey-haired officials, one of them clean-shaven, the other with a thin moustache. The letter with the French stamp was from the Conservatoire, calling Ravel in for a meeting.

The principal's default expression is sneering. Wire-frame glasses rest on his hook nose. "Well," the principal says to Ravel. "We've been meaning to thank you for entertaining George Gershwin. How did you find the experience?"

Ravel tries to smile. "Not a complete waste of time. The man is very charming."

"Glad to hear it," the principal says. "Part of your membership here, as you know, is to share the French experience with the New World. We've taken note of the pride you have for your practice, and a little savoir faire was all that was missing."

"Of course," Ravel says, acting untroubled. "A mutually beneficial exercise."

The professor with shaggy eyebrows holds out a cheque. "Your payment."

"Merci," Ravel says, slipping it in his waistcoat.

The official with the thin moustache begins to speak. "New works, Ravel... When shall we hear them?"

"We like to make plans for the coming season," the principal adds.

Ravel nods. "Oui, bien sûr. I have something that's nearly finished."

The principal leans in. "Tell us about it."

"Well," Ravel says, basking in the flattering sunlight of his patrons. "I could say that street traders will whistle the melody in the market. I could say that it will be danced at the ballet, as well as at the village fete. This would all be true. But this piece of music is beyond fashion and analysis. Criticism will not even graze it. It will speak for itself; it will reach out and touch the people, standing up for itself..."

As Ravel swaggers and showboats, eyebrows

rise across the table, climbing the scaffolds of deep forehead wrinkles. A look passes between the elderly gentlemen. Finally, when it seems Ravel would sooner run out of breath than finish his self-inflation, the principal clears his throat.

"D'accord," the principal says. "With new material in order, what of another performance with Monsieur Gershwin?"

Ravel smiles, waiting for the punchline. "Oh – You were serious?"

"Indeed," the principal nods. "The music Gershwin is writing. It is as you say, 'standing up for itself'. Gershwin has a premiere coming up, supposedly inspired by his time in Paris. Perhaps the *master* would learn from the fruits of *his* tutelage."

"Mon Dieú…" Ravel takes a breath. "You don't mean to suggest a trip to New York? It's been so long. I'm not sure I wouldn't get trampled… And the awful cuisine—"

The principal cuts in. "Monsieur Ravel, we shall put it simply. Going to New York will create a buzz… whipping up publicity for a concert upon your return. You see, Maurice, it's everything or nothing at all. The affair could be lucrative, that is, if you can surmount your reluctance to travel. We're keen to see you through it…"

Ravel huffs, averting his eyes for a split second, then glaring with bold defiance at the principal. "How keen exactly?"

***

Returning home, Ravel stomps through the yard, cursing and cutting the air to ribbons with flailing arms. Aimée hears him coming and heads out to meet him with a double-cheek kiss. Ravel continues to bluster and complain, moving quickly inside to the kitchen where he hastily pours himself a glass of water.

"Maurice," Aimée says. "Que s'est-il passé?" She follows him inside.

"Oh nothing," Ravel crows, swinging the glass of water with wild abandon. Aimée dodges out of the splash-zone, bracing for more theatricals.

Ravel starts bellowing. "Why do I have to answer to those tweed-wrapped buffoons?" Draining the glass of water, he fishes in his pocket.

He clatters the glass down on the counter, then passes a crumpled piece of paper to Aimée. "Take care of this."

Aimée unfolds the heavily creased cheque. "I'll have trouble cashing it."

"Have it pressed for all I care!" Ravel fumes. "Those dilettante cronies take me for a puppet. Watching those bullfrog necks start wobbling… it boils my blood. With their stuffed shirts and garish moustachery. After my new piece, I'll have no need for them. I'll go over their bald heads and touch the people!"

Instead of preparing for his premiere of 'El Bolero', Ravel takes the next few days doing nothing but search for Debussy's slippers. Huffing around the chateau, he remains deaf to Aimée's attempts to soothe and divert him.

"Where *are* they?" he asks himself, having turned his entire closet out.

Aimée appears with a pair of slippers. "Here you go."

"Not those," he grumbles. "They make my feet swell. Gershwin must have stolen the slippers… Using them now to advance his career!"

"Do you even hear yourself?" Aimée asks. "Why would George take a pair of your slippers?"

Ravel glares at her. "Perhaps he didn't know until he unpacked. And now… he likes what he has."

Aimée sighs and shakes her head. "I've never heard anything so absurd. You need to get ready for the concert."

***

That evening at the premiere, Ravel sits with Aimée in his private box, listening to the final flourish of 'El Bolero'. After a half-second of silence, a woman cheers from the box beside Ravel's. Throughout the auditorium, the audience is divided. Many are grumbling with disappointment, and a few are even booing. Two boxes down from his own, Ravel spies Les Six. They're peering over at him, applauding facetiously, smirking and laughing.

A woman at the front of Ravel's box turns to him. "I'm quivering… it was explosive! Erotic!"

Ravel tries to look modest and grateful, bowing

his head to the woman with a forced smile. She gives a little curtsy and begins to collect her things. Although her praise was genuine, and mirrored in about half the audience, this is not the clarified consensus Ravel had hoped for.

He points out a jeering old lady in another box. "Well, Aimée... *She* got the message!"

Aimée sighs. "If that's the response you wanted, I don't understand going through this at all."

"That was appalling!" the old lady shouts from across the concert hall.

Before Ravel can join in the shouting match, Les Six burst into the box. The whole lot of them — Auric, Durey, Honegger, Milhaud, Poulenc and Tailleferre.

"Ah, Les Pricks," Ravel says mockingly. "I bet you're loving this, aren't you? This will be the source of many a Conservatoire joke..."

Milhaud takes the lead. "Au contraire, Ravel! You should be very proud! Have some champagne."

The others hang back near the entrance to the box, but Honegger steps forward with a sweeping hand gesture. "Really, Ravel. Look how you divided the audience; masterful!"

Ravel pretends to play along, raging inwardly.

Aubrik pipes up. "Such a picture-postcard melody. So lame and repetitive. Yet you bludgeon them with it until they can't reject the – what is the word? *Merde*. Until they can't reject the *shit*. They have to embrace it!"

Honegger cackles. "And then they wallow in it! But I know what *Maurice* Antoinette will say – 'Let them eat shit!'"

Milhaud chuckles. "Maurice, you dark horse. We congratulate you!"

Ravel takes a sip of champagne, trying to show a tranquil exterior. "Monsieurs, this is music for our time. It may not be a typical three-movement concerto, but I know what the public deserves, and I've simply showed up to provide that."

"Well said! A man of the people," Milhaud mocks.

Honegger leans in to clink glasses with Ravel, connecting so hard that his own glass breaks. "Oh my!" Honnegger laughs, shaking champagne from his hand.

"Don't be so heavy-handed," Aubrik says from the door. "You're no Maurice Ravel."

Ravel's jaw trembles as he tries to stay composed. Slowly, he sets down his glass on the railing, then brushes the spilled drops of champagne from his dinner jacket.

"Well that was really suave," Aimée mutters, glaring at Honegger.

"Well done, Maurice," Honegger says, ignoring Aimée. "Now on to New York!"

Before Ravel can respond, Les Six are leaving the box, calling in someone to clean up the glass. Ravel waves a hand to bid them adieu, turning to lean over the railing and think. He can't believe Les Six would still want him to go to New York. Could they only hope to further humiliate him upon return? Will the New York venture only cheapen the status of his music by association with American kitsch? Ravel worries he's made a terrible mistake by agreeing to the trip. He gives Aimée a nervous glance, then turns back to the emptying auditorium, thoughts awhirl in his head.

CHAPTER 12

George and Kitty are under the sheets, moaning softly and making dispassionate love. George looks around with a worn, glazed expression, surveying the objects in his bedroom rather than Kitty. Nevertheless, the deed is done, and they fall into each other's arms. George feels somewhat relaxed, if only for a moment.

Kitty lights up. "Well, that was… fine I guess." She rolls over to face him.

"I'm sorry," George says. "I know it's been better before."

"I don't see why you push yourself so hard," she says. "You have a right to cut loose."

George lights a cigarette of his own. "My mind is on other things."

"Like what?" she asks, blowing the smoke sideways.

"They won't let me write music how I want to write it," he says. "They keep telling me not to make it so alternative. Not to *overdo* it."

Kitty takes a drag. "Is that what you were doing in France? Overdoing it?"

George blows smoke from the corner of his mouth. He watches her face for a moment, wondering if she could have heard about Aimée. "No, Kitty. If anything, Ravel had me strip things down, until there was no way to overdo anything. This isn't something I picked up in France. It's an urge I've had for a long time."

Kitty strokes his hair sympathetically.

George sighs and stubs out his cigarette. "You say I should cut loose. Well, Ira says I should rest. He thinks I'm burning out."

Kitty lets smoke unfurl from her nose, even as she takes another drag. "Ira... first he's your brother who behaves like your mother, now he's your doctor as well?"

George flicks on the bedside lamp. "Very funny, Kitty." He holds out the ashtray for Kitty's cigarette, then takes it over to the can in the corner and bangs it out.

"You'll be okay George," Kitty says. "As long as you let me keep an eye on you."

George flicks off the light again and the streetlamps spill in, mixing with soft rays of moonlight. He cradles Kitty in his arms and shuts his eyes. Kitty smokes one more cigarette, then falls asleep on George's chest.

In the morning, Kitty is quietly dreaming, but George lies awake. With his pink-rimmed and bloodshot eyes, he looks as though he hasn't slept a wink. A knock comes at the door, and he bolts upright.

Ira calls in. "Up and at 'em, brother. I brought bagels."

George pulls on a pair of socks, then slides into a robe. He kisses Kitty's cheek then goes out to the living room, shutting the door as softly as he can. Seeing no sign of Ira, he heads to the Frigidaire for a yogurt.

Ira bursts in the front door, followed by two burly workmen. Startled, George manages to hold onto his yogurt cup.

Ira chuckles at George's wide-eyed stare. "Had to let these fellows in. Did ya' sleep well?" Ira takes a bagel from the paper bag on the table, spreading cream cheese and slapping on lox and pickled onions. "Make sure you're getting seven hours. Me… I gotta get off before Leonore, or else I'm listening to a wounded buffalo all night."

George takes a bite of his yogurt, still in a sleepless daze. He glances at the workmen and it all comes back. "Moving… Oh, no." George slaps a hand to his face. "I haven't started packing."

Ira looks up from a mouthful of bagel. "That's why we're here!"

The two men give George a thumbs-up.

Ira swallows half the bagel in a single bite, then claps his hands, setting off a ringing in George's ears. Just as he doubles over, groping for support on the kitchen table, Kitty strolls in, stark naked and bold as ever. She walks to the Frigidaire and takes out an apple. Staring at the workmen, she takes a crunchy bite.

Everyone gawks, except George, who's rubbing his temples. When he finally notices the palpable silence, he looks up. "Kitty… what are you—"

"I was hungry," Kitty says, taking another bite of her apple, then turning to the Frigidaire again, searching for something more substantial.

George turns to the workmen, his colour high.

"Do you fellas mind waiting outside?"

The two workmen are frozen to the spot.

"Hey!" Ira shouts, snapping his fingers. "Move it!"

Kitty turns to squint at the kitchen table. "Bagels?" she asks.

"Yes ma'am…" one of the workmen says, and Ira promptly shoes him out.

George turns to Kitty, open-mouthed and struggling for words.

"Morning," Kitty says. "Gonna butter my bagel, or should I have your brother do it?" She crosses her arms over her breasts, tapping her foot.

Before George can speak, Ira returns. "Well, the great Kitty Carlisle!"

"Ira Gershwin, thanks for breakfast. It's more than I can expect from your brother." Kitty winks, grabs the entire bag of bagels, then sashays off to George's bedroom.

Ira leans over to George. "So, you *didn't* get seven hours."

***

George paces about in his new apartment. Much more refined than the East Village two-bedroom, this is a one-bedroom in Yorkville, just for George alone – no longer a crash pad for Ira when he isn't with his wife, Leonore.

While George frets about where to put the piano, Ira and Leonore are chatting in the living room. As of this late afternoon hour, they're both nearly fed up with George's laborious moving methods.

When Ira finishes some gripe or another about his stubborn and finicky brother, Leonore changes the subject. "Would you look at the size of this living room? This is twice the size of ours. What does George need with a room this size? There's only one of him, after all."

"Entertaining, I suppose," Ira says.

They both laugh, then check to make sure George hasn't heard them.

Leonore admires the wainscoting and crown mouldings. "Are you sure we signed for the right property?"

George pops his head in from the bedroom. "Have you got any candles? I need candles in every room."

"Whaddya need with candles?" Ira asks. "You'll ruin your eyes with candles…"

"I must have candles," George says, without any humour in his voice.

Ira and Leonore exchange looks.

"I can get you candles," Ira says. "Just don't compose by them. Or read or write… or really do anything with them, except for… you know what, I guess." He turns to his wife. "Honey, would you go down the street and see if we have any spares?"

"No problem," Leonore says, rolling her eyes when she walks out. "Candles… right away," she mutters.

George ducks into the bedroom and Ira follows.

"The bedroom's nearly as big as the living room," Ira says. "Can't imagine how you found this place for such a price. Oh wait…" he says with saccharine sarcasm, "You didn't."

"Mm-hmm," George says. "Forever in your debt, brother. Now quit prattling on and help me with this." George has a grip on a funny-looking stool, and Ira helps him jam it beneath an armoire.

"You gonna be able to get that out later?" Ira

asks.

George ignores him, ripping open a cardboard box with a pocketknife.

"You know," Ira says, walking over to look at the view of the East River, "I think Porgy will be our crowning achievement."

George turns to Ira with a smile, but says nothing. He's far more excited about *An American in Paris* than he is about *Porgy and Bess*. But he knows it's a bad time to tell his brother about it.

"Broadway hasn't seen anything like it," Ira says. "I just *know* the critics will be singing our praises."

George mutters an "Mm-hmm," and continues to rip open boxes.

Ira sighs and decides to help his brother unpack. He heads for a pile of suitcases in the corner. At the top of the heap is a tattered leather trunk. Ira takes hold of it and nearly throws it through the picture window.

"Yecch," Ira says, putting the case back and holding his nose. "What's that ungodly smell?"

George is still focused on his pile of cardboard boxes. "Those worthless lackeys, they didn't even label the boxes! This is glassware..." He spins to face Ira. "Glassware! Why is the glassware in the bedroom?"

Ira shrugs, pointing to the tattered trunk with a questioning look. "Something you picked up in Paris?" he asks.

"Maybe," George says. "Open it."

Ira covers his mouth and nose with a handkerchief, and unlatches the trunk. An even more oppressive aroma expands into the room when the trunk is open.

Ira coughs, and George can't help but turn his head, detecting the odour as well.

"My God, these are your slippers?" Ira says through his pinched nose. "I certainly don't remember packing them."

George glances back at his brother for a split second. "Then I must've packed that trunk," he mutters.

Ira drops the trunk on the floor, afraid to touch the slippers inside.

Next on the luggage pile is a slender black briefcase, which Ira has seen George carry his compositions in. Forgetting the foul-smelling slippers, he opens the briefcase instead, pulling out a few sheets of paper.

An American in Paris is scribbled at the top, half-erased in faded pencil.

"Aha!" Ira says, triumphant, despite his nosiness. "What's this you've been hiding?"

George takes note of his brother's tone and whirls around. "It's just a little side project... something I've been working on."

"Well," Ira says, intrigued. "Then hum it to me. How does it go?"

George heaves a sigh and goes over to the window, stretching out his hand for Ira to give him the score. "I appreciate your interest, but it's really not finished, and that's an old draft, besides."

Ira hands over the composition. "If it's not finished, then maybe I can help. I just need the general idea of how it goes—"

George cuts him off. "Ira, give it up. I'm sorry, but it's not a lyrical thing. It's a piece. Not even a song. Something that almost comes close to a concerto..." George turns away, flushing red. "It doesn't work with lyrics. It's too long."

Ira lets up, trying not to sound disappointed.

"Okay, brother, if you say so."

"Sorry," George says. "I can tell you more when I'm further along."

Ira perks up again. "Did you show it to Ravel?"

"No," George says, going back to his moving boxes.

"Well that makes me feel better." Ira turns back to the frail trunk, giving it a little kick. The slippers wobble inside. Ira covers his mouth again, taking a second look. "All right then, what's with these godawful slippers? They can't belong to a brother of mine."

George mutters something inaudible.

"Just a minute," Ira says with sudden realisation. "Only an old man would hold onto something like this. Do they belong to Ravel? Some kind of souvenir fetish?"

"Don't be ridiculous!" George cries.

Ira can see that he's struck a nerve. He crosses his arms and approaches his brother. "George... don't get hot-tempered over some old slippers. There's something special about them, isn't there? Just what are you playing at?"

George wipes the sweat from his brow. "They

aren't Ravel's slippers. They belonged to Claude Debussy."

Ira's eyebrows catapult to the top of his forehead. "No wonder they smell so wretched! They belonged to a man who's dead and buried!"

George takes a breath, but offers no response.

"So where did you get them?" Ira asks.

George shrugs. "This is the first that I've seen them, ever since Ravel showed them to me in Paris."

Ira takes on the look of a detective, hot on the trail of some devious motive. "So... if this trunk belongs to Ravel, then how did it end up in a pile of your luggage?"

George turns back to moving his boxes. "Your guess is as good as mine, brother."

Ira goes over to where George is unpacking. He leans against a set of drawers wrapped in a protective blanket. "George Gershwin is no thief. So, from what you're *not* saying, I think you *must* think your luggage got mixed up somehow."

"It's entirely possible," George says drily, clearly ready to move on.

Ira clicks his tongue. "Well, then, I'm guessing

you'll want to send them back."

"Sure, Ira. But it's not a big-ticket item on my list. It's just a pair of old slippers."

"But they belonged to *Debussy*," Ira retorts.

George gives his brother a withering look, then takes a box of cutlery into the kitchen. Ira follows, so George puts the box down with a sigh, then walks over to the bay window in the living room. Ira follows with the same dead-eye Dick look on his face. George starts fiddling with the curtains, muttering about how cheap they are.

Ira leans back on the windowsill and clears his throat. "George... Why do I get the funny feeling you want to keep the repugnant slippers?"

George goes on about the drapery, under his breath.

"It just seems a little odd," Ira says. "But I suppose I can't make you give them back."

George lets go of the curtain and turns to Ira. "I'm giving them back, don't worry. I just now found out I had them, so there are no funny feelings to have..."

Ira grins. "Say... when you ditched me in Paris, you really got around, huh?"

George shakes his head and looks out the window at his brand-new view. Tugboats and barges are stitching their way along the river. Ira can see his brother's reflection in the glass. There's a hint of a smile on George's lips.

Next moment, the front door opens and Leonore calls out. "Candle delivery for George Gershwin! Your oh-so-vital candles."

George turns to Ira. "Go on, Ira. I need a minute here to unpack by myself. Bring the candles in a couple minutes, and I'll tell you a story about 'getting around' in Paris." The hint of a smile is now a full-fledged grin.

Ira nods. "Consider it done. This room will soon be candle-ridden."

George goes back to moving his boxes, while Ira heads out to meet Leonore in the living room.

***

A few hours later, the sky has gone black, and George is alone in his new apartment. He's hunched over the piano keys, at work on *An American in Paris*. Next moment, the phone rings, jolting him out of focus. With an irritated glance, he wills the phone to stop ringing. Nothing doing.

"Who could that be…?" he mutters to himself, determined to ignore the call. But the phone keeps ringing, so George makes a few final notes in his composition pages, then gets up in a tizzy. Ira had the phone installed ahead of the move-in date, and now George is cursing him for it.

George grumbles over to the side table by the front door, where he takes up the receiver. "Hello?"

"Long distance from France," the operator says. "Do you accept?"

"France…" George drifts off for a moment, considering who it could be.

The operator's voice again. "Sir? Still there?"

"Oh!" George shouts, realising at once who it could be. "Maurice? Is it Ravel?"

"The accent was heavy, Sir," the operator says, a little annoyed. "It might have been Ravine… But surely it was a man's voice. Shall I put it through?"

"Yes, yes," George says, sitting down in the seat beside the phone.

After a long dial tone, the connection crackles

to life.

"Hello?" The distant, tinny voice of Maurice Ravel.

"Maurice!" George says eagerly. "My God, how are you doing?"

"Just fine," Ravel says after a moment's pause, the time it takes for the signal to cross back over the ocean.

"That's great!" George says, crossing his legs and reaching hopefully for a notepad and pen, in case Ravel offers him any advice.

"So, George, er…" Ravel falters. "How is New York?"

"All right, I suppose," George sighs. "I'm working on a piece I like, but I'm supposed to be working on some Broadway drivel instead."

"Ah, you poor man," Ravel drawls. "What a waste of a mind."

George lets the backhanded compliment slide. He switches the receiver to the other ear and purses his lips.

"Anyway," Ravel continues, "I'm just double-checking on the matter we posted you about. Are you quite sure there wasn't a luggage mix-up? You know those oafs at the station…"

"Yeah," George says. "Like I said in the letter back, I looked over my baggage, and nothing was out of order."

"Oh, really?" The long-distance connection begins to waffle. Although George wants to keep talking with his mentor, he also realises that if Ravel won't drop the matter, he can always ring off and blame the connection.

"Anything in particular you might have lost?" George asks, knowing full-well which trunk Ravel is searching for, and what it contains. He decides to toy with his mentor awhile, try the slippers out for himself, then return them in due time.

"Oh, just a few items I can't find…" Ravel pauses. "Ever since we left for Berlin."

"Oh yeah?" George asks. "You lost some scores?"

"No, no," Ravel says. "Just some little things, personal items."

"What, your earplugs?" George asks.

"What? No, not ear plugs…"

"Well then," George says. "What little things?"

Pure silence between them.

Finally, Ravel exhales on the other line. "I'm coming to New York."

"Ha!" George exclaims. "Looks like I got something out of Europe after all... Or, should I say, some*one.*"

"Yes, well," Ravel says. Perhaps you made a stronger impression than I first anticipated. The Conservatoire is supporting the trip. We should meet when I arrive. I know you'll have a new... performance opening soon. I'd like to attend. Maybe we can even arrange some sort of performance for us as well."

George lights up. "We can perform this new piece I have! 'An American—'"

Even with the intercontinental delay, Ravel cuts in before George can finish. "Let's not discuss it now. What do you Americans say, 'jumping the gun?'. Anyway George, I'm pleased to have been an aid to you."

Tension hangs between them for a moment, but George decides to let it go. "Right, this is long distance... We can plan the performance in person."

"Indeed," Ravel says. "I'll be in touch when I arrive in the city. Goodbye, George."

"But when...?" George tries to ask, but the line goes dead.

George buzzes with excitement as he sets down the receiver. If he's going to give back the slippers when Ravel gets to New York, he might as well make use of them in the meantime. He goes to his bedroom and tries them on for the first time, pinching his nose at the stench. He lights a scented candle and sets it atop the piano. The slippers move with self-assurance on the foot pedals, as George Gershwin returns to his score with a newfound urgency.

***

As the days wear on, George goes to various meetings with movers and shakers in the music business. At Ira's suggestion, he does his best to maintain his status as a prominent American composer. Rubbing elbows with some of the industry's big players, he feels his career taking off in a major way, although he still wishes he had more time for writing new music, namely, *An American in Paris*, which still needs a few finishing touches.

One morning, George has breakfast with Walter Damrosch, the conductor of the New York Symphony. Damrosch is a seasoned patron of the arts, specifically when it comes to modern music, and George feels he can trust Damrosch with the alternative themes of *An American in Paris*. Gershwin tells Damrosch about his plans for the concert debut.

"I'm intrigued," Damrosch says. "I've been waiting years for something like this. And I'm happy it's coming from you, with such an impressive catalogue already."

George smiles, "I think you'll be vindicated with this one."

"Well, when can I hear it? You must come up to the house," he says. "Margaret and I would love to have you. I've already written to you several times."

"I know, I know, I'm behind on correspondence. Just as soon as it's finished," George says. "I don't want you to have to tidy up my sketches again."

Damrosch waves a hand. "So, come up and work on it! I won't give you any advice you don't ask for. But it helps to have another set of ears, no? You can come up for a whole weekend. A week! Whatever time you need."

"It sounds perfect," George says. "But I've got a schedule like you wouldn't believe. Just this afternoon we have a photoshoot with *Time Magazine*."

"Ah well," Damrosch says, sipping an espresso. "Publicity. Must grease the wheels of the media machine. Anyway, we've heard that Ravel is coming here. We think the two of you should play Carnegie Hall, together... and backed up by the philharmonic, of course."

"Oh," George sets down his cup. "Well, yes, I mean... Sure! That'd be—"

"Splendid?" Damrosch asks.

"Oh yes," George says. "Fantastic. But... How will you propose it to Ravel?"

Damrosch tips George a wink, possessing an aristocratic air. "You let me handle it... All I can say is it comes down to publicity." Damrosch gestures as if setting type for a newspaper. "Two musical titans… a meeting of the artistic minds! Ravel wants that sort of headline as much as you. Otherwise, why come all the way from Paris?"

George raises his cup and clinks it with Damrosch.

"Let's make it happen," George says. "I can't wait."

***

Later that same day, George and Ira are waiting around at the photoshoot for *Time Magazine*. The stylist has them in golfing attire, complete with plus-four knickerbockers, argyle vests and collared white shirts. The photographer is posing them around on a false green with a backdrop of blue sky and puffy clouds.

"I got a letter from Heyward," Ira says.

George turns to him. "That so?"

Ira sets his club aside and moves closer to George, casting a glance about the room. "Get this – Al Jolson is bidding to fund the rest of Porgy!"

"Oh," George gasps, then looks around, toning down his reaction. "But they'll give him the starring role if that happens!"

"Precisely…" Ira says with a little sigh. "But it's a whole lot of bacon…"

George is having trouble controlling his reaction, looking around nervously while keeping his voice low, yet emphatic. "Jolson will ruin it," he says to Ira. "What's with Heyward? Why's he talking to Jolson?"

Ira shakes his head. "Dubose Heyward is hard up. Spent the better part of last year adapting it for the stage…"

"Must not have been making any dough on the side," George says. "Poor writers…"

"You're telling me!" Ira says, catching the eye of the prop-man. He drops back to a whisper. "So now he's cash-poor. Besides, Jolson's a butter-and-egg man. Guy with some actual-factual long green. Can you blame him?"

"No," George sighs, "I suppose not. But Jolson as a blacked-up Porgy, can you imagine? The crowd's gonna crack up, even at the serious parts! Heyward's gonna be dragged through the mud…"

Ira clicks his tongue. There's a twinkle in his eye. "We'll step in, brother. Promise an all-black cast and Heyward will go with us. Are you ready?"

George nods quickly. "If it's gonna keep Jolson from grubbing it up… yeah, cancel my plans. I'm all yours."

The photographer breaks in. "Sorry, gents, had to reload the canisters, now we got fresh bulbs and a new roll. Time to make the magic. Ever done a front-cover shoot? I doubt it! Ira, you hold the flag while George putts."

Ira grins and gives a jovial salute, then lifts the flag while George crouches down to line up his shot.

The photographer snaps two shots then passes the camera. His assistant barely catches it before the heavy Yashica falls to the false turf. A buzzing remains in the air from the hot flashbulbs.

"Now then," the photographer says, twirling a trendy moustache, "let's have big brother step aside…"

"Oh, sure!" Ira says, beaming. When he steps off the stage he calls up to George, cupping his mouth so the whole studio hears him. "There you go George! That should be enough room for your head now!"

George smiles candidly and the photographer clicks the shutter. The hot lights flash, and the good-natured brotherly taunting is etched in time.

***

The following week, George, Ira, Todd Duncan and his wife, Gladys, are upstairs in the attic of Ira's apartment building. They've been rehearsing in the tiny attic space, because there are no phones to distract them. The little room is big enough to accommodate five or so people at maximum, and it's so out of the way that almost nobody knocks on the trap door.

The Al Jolson problem has been taken care of, and George and Ira are trying to recruit Todd Duncan for the role of Porgy. George is playing the banjo and Ira is singing, running through 'I Got Plenty O' Nuttin''. At the first crescendo, Ira starts crooning in a terrible South Carolina accent.

Todd and Gladys exchange looks, their jaws hanging low.

"You hear that, Todd?" Ira shouts over an instrumental break. "This song is gonna make you a star!"

By the final chorus, Ira's reedy voice reaches its limits. Todd and Gladys are cringing, yet can't help smiling at Ira's expense. Ira is too focused on shrieking the final lyrics to notice their reactions. Suddenly, the latch pops on the trap door, and Leonore appears on the ladder. George stops playing and everyone turns to face her.

"Ira," Leonore says, "Sorry to break in... But there's—"

"Leonore. Is it really so vital...?" Ira trails off, then turns to Todd and Gladys. "I'm sure it will just be a moment."

Ira sets the banjo aside, then crouches down at the trap door, where he and his wife whisper in low tones. Ira's voice is calm and much steadier than Leonore's, but the others in the room can't make out what's being said.

Todd shrugs at Gladys, who makes a flat, emotionless smile with her painted lips.

"All right, I promise. I'll check up on it later." Ira says, and Leonore descends the ladder. Ira slides the bolt on the latch, then straightens up. "Back to it, then?"

"What'd she say?" George asks. "Whatsa matter?

"Oh nothing," Ira says, casting a reassuring glance about the room. "Come now, once more from the top. Our esteemed guests deserve a full run-through." Ira starts flipping back to the first page of 'I Got Plenty Of Nuttin''.

"It had to be something," George says drily.

"Well," Ira says in a conciliatory tone. "It's finished now, no need to worry —"

George cuts him off. "No. That's it. That's the last interruption I can take. No more. I'm done." He gets up from the piano and goes to the trap door, where he starts to fiddle with the latch, his hands shaking. "Damn thing's stuck again..."

Ira laughs, taking his brother's reaction as some kind of joke.

George pulls hard on the latch, nicking his thumb in recoil. He curses, then with an apologetic glance at Gladys and Todd, he begins glaring at Ira. "You know, *brother*, nobody has asked me..."

"Nobody's asked you what?" Ira asks, incredulous. "What on earth are you getting at?"

"Not a single person," George says impetuously,

"has asked for a piece to be written since I got back from Paris."

"Oh… shoot." Ira snaps his fingers. "Well, sure… Because you haven't been available. With all the upcoming shows…"

"I don't want to play Broadway all the time!" George yells, acting more and more childishly.

Ira's mouth hangs open for a half-second. "I beg your pardon?" He turns to Todd and Gladys. "Would you give us a moment?"

"Sure," Todd replies, delicately taking his wife's hand. "Well, from that particular number, it was… well…" He doesn't seem to have the right words.

"The song by itself is strange," Ira explains, "but in the context of the whole show, you'll see. Just a minute while I confer with the genius behind the music…"

"No trouble, Mr Gershwin," Todd says, leading his wife to the trap door. George shuffles out of the way, hanging his head in a sulky manner. Todd slides the latch out carefully and easily, and he and Gladys disappear through the hatch without a word.

George makes to follow them down, but Ira puts a hand on his brother's shoulder. "Look, George. Take shots at my work if you want to. I know Porgy wasn't your idea, so I understand if it feels like playing second fiddle—"

"Fiddle positions have never mattered!" George cries, getting up to his feet. "Not now, not ever. You're missing the point!" He wags a fist at his brother. "I shouldn't have to yell from the top of a mountain to get commissions! You know how fuckin' famous I am? They're taking my picture for *Time Magazine*, and still I've got no Janus. Just the same whores lining up for their bit parts... in the same Broadway drivel we've always done!"

"Janus?" Ira asks. "Her again? George, you're a musical genius. The women are a thousand times prettier in California. You wanna ditch Broadway and pick out a movie star, then let's leave New York to the urchins like Al Jolson. Hollywood, brother... the land of milk and honey... the silver screen. Whaddya say?"

"No!" George shouts, tugging at his hair, messing up his grease-combed look. "I *will* do Porgy... I think Porgy is just fine, but I want something more…"

"Something more?" Ira asks, trying his best to understand.

George shakes his head. "It doesn't matter. You can't help me anyway."

"We can't give up on this show, George," Ira says.

"Then don't start talking about the next one. No more after this," George says. "Okay? Porgy is the last Broadway gig for a while. I need another break. Paris was good, but it wasn't long enough. And even then, Wally took me out when I was just getting started."

Ira nods politely, waiting for George to go on.

George looks back at his brother in silence, searching his eyes and making sure he's been listening. "I need something I can call my own," George finally says.

"After Porgy," Ira says. "Yes, George. Then we talk."

"After Porgy we make a *change*," George says, gritting his teeth resolutely. "And I mean a real, radical change for both of us."

Ira nods. "Okay, brother."

George narrows his eyes for a split second, then at last seems to relax. He nods curtly and goes back to the piano. Ira leans down through the trap door and hollers for Todd and Gladys to come up, then he picks up the banjo and they start in from the top, playing just the instrumental as they await the return of Todd and Gladys.

CHAPTER 13

A few weeks later, Ravel arrives in New York. Walter Damrosch has arranged to collect him, pulling up at the airport in a luxury motor car. A chauffeur sits in the front seat, ready to help with Ravel's bags when they spot him at the kerb side.

Damrosch spies him first and gets out to wave him over. "Maurice Ravel!" he calls.

Ravel shuffles over, leaving his bags for the airport staff and the chauffeur.

Damrosch meets him halfway, pumping his hand with excitement. "Lovely to see you here in the big apple, Monsieur Ravel."

"Herr Damrosch," Ravel says, "the pleasure is mine. But I hardly slept on the flight, so I hope you don't expect too much Parisian charm right away."

"Does Paris have charm? I didn't know!" Damrosch laughs.

Ravel joins in laughter. Damrosch is one of

the few people who needn't earn respect from Ravel. His rise in the world of classical music was patient and humble, driven more by talent than slick-talk or networking. Now Damrosch held the formidable position of conductor at the New York Symphony Orchestra, a title which sharpened his image even further, especially in Ravel's eyes.

On the way to the Gramercy Park Hotel, Damrosch informs Ravel of the radio broadcast recording set for tomorrow.

"Gershwin on the radio?" Ravel asks. "Well… it could be interesting."

Damrosch smiles. "I know it's your first full evening in town, but I promise… You won't want to miss it."

"I haven't any other plans," Ravel says mildly.

"Well then, it's settled," Damrosch says happily. "I'll pick you up here around four o'clock. It's at the NBC building, so I thought we'd get an early dinner beforehand. Wonderful restaurants in the area."

Ravel nods, looking as though food is the last thing on his mind. "Sure, very well."

"You must be tired. Not to worry. You can

sleep until the afternoon and still be on time. You know, Gershwin has only improved since you played with him in Berlin. You must've made an impression."

"That so?" Ravel asks.

"With this new piece he's premiering," Damrosch says. "His writing has *really* developed."

Ravel turns to Damrosch with a drowsy look. "What's it called?"

Damrosch grins. "You'll like this – *An American in Paris*. Do you believe it?"

"Ah…" Ravel says, a phantom smile almost crossing his lips.

"It'll be the centrepiece of the evening," Damrosch explains. "I'll be intrigued to hear what you make of it. And – He's conducting it himself!"

"Conducting?" Ravel looks flummoxed. "But he's a pianist. Is he conducting from a piano?"

Damrosch chuckles. "Well, I mustn't give the game away, must I, Maurice?"

Ravel can't help but be intrigued, and a big smile spreads over his face this time. "I suppose not, Walter."

Damrosch smiles back. "But I will tell you this –

piano or rostrum, the audience won't know where he's conducting from… They won't have to."

Ravel frowns, still clouded from jet lag. "Won't have to? Oh! Because it's on the radio!"

"Precisely," Damrosch says. "If you ask me, I've got big hopes for radio. It'll be good for George to premiere it this way. Invisible electronic waves, broadcast to as many stations as possible, relaying the signal on and on to others. Radio… it's an opportunity to educate. To bring people wonderful recordings they wouldn't normally hear."

Ravel starts to zone out. As a veteran ranter himself, he knows when one's coming.

"Soon we'll have a radio hour for school children, and the NBC will give out textbooks for teachers who want to help their students with music appreciation. The comprehension for classical music must be preserved, and the young people are simply rapt by the radio. What a way to reach the youth!"

Ravel nods with token understanding, watching the skyscrapers whip past the window. He mutters 'yes' or 'uh-huh' or 'oh, really' at the right times, while Damrosch details the merits of the ground-breaking medium.

***

The next evening, Rudy Vallée, Ravel, Ira and George sit in a small recording booth at the NBC radio studio, setting up for the radio premiere. An 'On Air' sign is poised overhead, but still dark. A chamber orchestra is assembled beyond a soundproof glass, tuning up for the performance. Rudy makes chit-chat with the guests, then finally gives them a ten-second countdown, after which the 'On Air' light begins to glow red.

After a round of introductions, Rudy starts with a softball question for George. "Here's a query you both must have to encounter a couple times a week, so it should be an easy one. When you work with your brother, which comes first: the words or the music?"

"The contract!" Ira interrupts, before George can answer.

Rudy chuckles politely, and the rest of the room joins in, although somewhat falsely.

"Well," George says. "It's usually the music. I hit on a new tune, fix it up and play it for Ira. Then he gets an idea for lyrics, and we iron it out together."

Rudy smiles. "Bravo, brothers. A tried and true method, and it certainly has gotten you far. Now George, how did you get started in music?"

"Well," George replies. "I left high school to take a job as a song plugger at Remick's. Fifteen bucks a week."

"Small potatoes," Rudy says. "But you gotta eat! Okay then, how much money do you make now, George? Gotta be more than that…"

George chuckles. "About half as much as you do. Hey Rudy, you do the math, how much is that?"

"One third as much as I told you this afternoon!" Rudy quips, and the whole room laughs in genuine amusement. "One more question now, George. Which one of your show tunes is better than all the rest, top of the heap?"

George pauses a moment to look down at the basic script for the show. Finding his line, he looks back at Rudy. "Out of all time?"

"All time!" Rudy declares. "The whole jumpin' catalogue."

"Well then, Rudy," George says jovially. "It's gotta be this one!" George goes to the muted piano in front of the plexiglass wall, where the lead violinist gives him an affirmative nod. The musicians wait for his cue from their soundproofed room. Waving his hands for a four-count lead-in, George starts in on, 'I Got Rhythm', and the chamber orchestra follows with a sonorous bellow of strings.

After the first measure, Rudy turns to Ravel. "And how about our guest from overseas? Whaddya think?"

Ravel isn't sure what to say. He's too nervous being packed into the tiny radio recording booth.

Rudy buys him a little time. "If you're just tuning in, this is Maurice Ravel, the great French composer, here at the NBC radio studio. And he's got an opinion on 'I Got Rhythm', the George Gershwin original from the classic Broadway show, *Girl Crazy!* What about it, Ravel, are you crazy for this one?"

"It's... fantastique!" Ravel says, hoping his false tone isn't picked up by the microphone.

"That it is," Rudy says cheerfully. "And coming from Mr Ravel, what a compliment! You've picked the right station, listeners. Right now, the one and only George Gershwin is playing one of his best original tunes. This one's called 'I Got Rhythm'. Don't switch the dial, you're in for something really special. Sit back and see if you got some rhythm, too. Right here on NBC radio live."

Ravel covers his microphone and leans over to Ira, who takes off one of his headphones. "Mon Dieú," Ravel whispers. "Is this absolutely necessary?"

"Of course," Ira whispers back. "It sells loads of sheet music."

Rudy chimes in again. "Coming up: more music from Brooklyn's very own George Gershwin. George and his brother Ira are both here in the studio. Both gentlemen occupy impressive positions, not only in writing top tunes for the Broadway stage, but several other creative fields as well. After a few brief messages from our sponsors, George Gershwin will bring us an exclusive, worldwide radio premiere. The new work is entitled, *An American in Paris*. This little number is Gershwin's Ode to city of lights – The trials and tribulations of a homesick American, walking the historic, uniquely-Parisian streets. A brand-new composition from America's leading composer, followed by more music and discussion with the Gershwin brothers. Coming up! Just after the break…"

The 'On Air' light flicks off, and a dim yellow bulb begins to glow on the mixing board, with 'Commercial Interlude' emblazoned below it. Rudy leans back in his swivel chair and laces his hands behind his head, regarding the group with a winning smile.

George finishes the measure at the arranged time, cutting off the orchestra with a wave and a swipe of his hand.

Rudy starts to clap and the other two follow suit. They each call out praises and George takes a small bow, blushing a little. Then he sits back down on the piano bench, facing the others.

Rudy leans forward in his chair. "Okay, George. Ready for the new one?"

"Born ready," George says, beaming.

***

The following day, Ravel rides along with George on Broadway, this time in a taxi instead of a luxury car. George points out the most striking landmarks, and Ravel soaks it all in, surprising himself with how happy he is to be here. He was dreading the pace of the city, and even though it's too fast for his liking, being here in this musical mecca makes up for it.

The cab drops them off at a tall brick building. Ravel looks up, marvelling at the height. Even the average buildings stretch up to the sky, as if compelled by a consensus of ambition, which Ravel can only describe to himself as distinctly American.

George follows his gaze, craning his neck. "Oh, yeah. Forty floors. Best place in my book to rehearse. But this ain't nothin'. Wait till you see Woolworth's. And the Chrysler building is gonna be even higher!"

George leads Ravel through the double doors and into a spacious lobby with a high ceiling.

George points up to it. "Used to be a hotel. I believe they remodelled it for offices around the turn of the century."

Ravel nods, mildly impressed with the informal trivia-tour.

George struts up to the young receptionist, with a wavy, Charleston bob secured by what looks like at least a dozen pins. George flirts with the young woman for a little too long, until she finally shoos him away to attend to another man waiting in line. George leaves with a wink and the jangle of keys, one for the elevator, and one for the rehearsal room.

He explains to Ravel on the way up how many ups and downs there have been while preparing for *Porgy and Bess*.

"Frankly," George says with an affected sigh, "I'll be able to relax after opening night, but the whole week leading up is just torture on the nerves."

The elevator bell chimes and George strides out into the hall, Ravel in tow. Without looking at all where he's going, Ravel has clearly been here a hundred times. Shutting the soundproofed door, George turns on his heel and strolls to the grand piano. "Make yourself at home," he calls out to Ravel over his shoulder.

Ravel goes peering around the room, which includes a small stage for the actors to assemble. For now it's an empty room, save for the two composers.

"Well," Ravel says. "Is it your happy place?"

George laughs. "You might say that. Best rehearsal room in the city. Just listen." He holds up a finger for a moment. "See?" George grins. "You could hear a pin drop."

"Unlike the city," Ravel says, looking out the window, where the blacktop streets are threaded with traffic, and the shifting shadows of clouds cover the ground, like a jigsaw-puzzle of natural forces, apparently indifferent to the footprint of man.

George nods. "New York City has never learned to be quiet."

"I could never make it a home," Ravel says. "How can you focus with all the… hullabaloo… is that the American term?"

George laughs again. "That's right. Hustle and bustle. Somehow, I manage. Growing up with it helps."

"Anyway, it doesn't matter," Ravel says. "I'm

not here to get comfortable. I'm here to give you a friendly eye. The tutelage I declined to provide you with before."

George takes a pause, lingering over the keys, then starts to settle the *Porgy and Bess* papers, putting them back in order on the music desk. All the while, he's wondering if Ravel's criticism will even be useful for this sort of project. With his classical training, will he even be able to make sense of it?

"What's wrong?" Ravel asks, taking a seat in the wooden folding chair.

"Oh," George says, snapping out of his private thoughts. "It's nothing, sorry. I just spaced out."

"Don't give me that look," Ravel says. "You think by teaching I'm only going to chastise you. Don't worry. That's not why I flew over the ocean. Wouldn't have been worth it. Vraiment, Mr Gershwin. I'm here to help, not to tear you down."

Ravel extends his hand.

George looks Ravel in the eye before shaking it, then with his free hand, he passes over Porgy in one single motion.

Ravel scans the first pages, "Ah, it's like you

say… Your mind is elsewhere."

"Okay, but have you seen the—" George tries to ask.

Ravel lifts a finger to keep George from talking. He flips through the rest of the songbook, dismay sinking into his expression with every page. "This looks just like how you came to me in Paris."

George's shoulders are slumped, and his head hangs low. "Well… it's a musical, so it has to at least follow a certain format… Even though," George perks up, "it is quite alternative for its time, not only in subject matter but composition… and instrumentation!"

Ravel watches George begin to ramble.

"If you knew Broadway theatre," George struggles to make his point, "then… I promise you. Then… you'd understand. It's… it's ahead of its time. Really it is."

Ravel stays quiet, so George tries a different tack. "How about I show you this other piece instead. I call it, *An American in Paris*."

"George," Ravel says evenly, tapping the sheaf of pages. "This is your next premiere. Why would we work on something else?"

"Well," George clarifies, "you might understand it better. The motivation…"

"This other one," Ravel says. "Is it a commissioned work?"

"No," George admits.

"Then it doesn't matter," Ravel says. "You're doing your brother's play. You can still bring it some more life. In fact, people expect it from you. Maybe you're right, I don't have a mind for this. But still, you must make it better, so that your moment on stage with *me* doesn't suffer either."

Ravel hands him the manuscript and gets up as if to leave, smirking to himself. George stares down at his music for a moment. All of a sudden, Ravel's words catch up to him.

"Wait," George says, "Did Damrosch convince you to play the duet?"

Ravel turns to face George. "I did not need convincing."

George gets up from the piano bench, excited beyond belief. "But wait, you haven't even heard the piece! Let's work on it now, it's called —"

Ravel cuts him off. "Not while your mind is clouded with…" Ravel peers over the pages in

George's hands. The title is hard to read upside-down. "…Porky in Bed."

"It's *Porgy*…" George says, "*Porgy and Bess*."

Ravel heads for the door, debating with himself whether to hold his tongue. He turns back and faces George again. At the expense of Gershwin's feelings, Ravel would rather make sure his point comes across.

"You know," Ravel says, "if you don't make some serious changes to that score, opening night may also be the closing one. Hear this, Mr Gershwin, before I let you go. Don't waste what you learned from me in Europe."

George is sick of being snubbed, tired of constantly having to prove himself. His face flushes red as a rhubarb pie, George strides up to Ravel at velocity. "I was wrong to ask for your help in the first place!"

Ravel sneers. "Indignant… Foolish boy!"

George takes a step back, still fuming, nonetheless. "Maybe you were never the legend I pegged you for."

Ravel laughs. "Such pithy remarks… Americans were never known for originality. Well, the illustrious George Gershwin is only a juvenile hobbyist, copying 'today's musical trend' and tinkering with quarter-notes like he tinkers with his—"

"Just leave then," George says, tossing up his hands.

Ravel nearly does, then tosses a final dagger. "I know what you did to Aimée."

George spins around, his colour drained.

Ravel's face is slack, devoid of expression. "The cruellest, most juvenile decision of all."

George has been gutted, but isn't quite ready to give up the fight. He straightens up. "What would you know about love, old man? All alone in the chateau, save for your servants. Frigid to anyone near you…"

Ravel grits his teeth. "Perhaps I'm no Casanova, but at least I don't use my celebrity on women. Having sex doesn't teach you the first thing about love. You know it, too. I can see the vacancy in your eyes, from all the conquests you cheated your way out of. You'll never be able to make real music, because those of us who can hear it, will only feel your emptiness."

George glares at his mentor, trying not to show the cracks in his pained expression.

Ravel sits back on his heels, knowing he has George on the ropes. "A Gershwin piece is just a bunch of instruments, going through the motions of melody and metre, sometimes taking a little gasp of spotlight, but never working in harmony. You write like a hollow-boned hummingbird... flitting from muse to muse with nothing that ever sticks."

George flares his nostrils, trying to stay calm. "And I win the hearts of millions," he says through his teeth.

"Yes," Ravel says. "Millions... But those who look deeper will see who you truly are. When they stop applauding, the effect is contagious. You're still young. You still have a chance to make a change."

Ravel turns to leave. "And if you don't believe me, just go and ask Aimée."

George feels an ice-pick of pain in his heart. Ravel steps into the hallway and shuts the door. The snap of the latch is a flintlock trigger in George's head, setting off a headache that clangs through his skull. His arms break out into channels of gooseflesh and his teeth start to chatter with full-body chills.

"Aimée…" he mutters to himself, pulling the piano cover over his shoulders, and collapsing to his knees with his head in his clutching hands.

CHAPTER 14

Less than a week later, *Porgy and Bess* opens on Broadway. The audience laughs in all the right places, shedding scattered tears in the moments of heartbreak. Young theatregoers leap out of their seats when the curtain comes down, and the slower-moving attendees get to their feet in due time, joining in a standing ovation.

Afterwards, George, Ira, and most of the cast and crew head for the Manhattan Club to celebrate. However, George can't focus on the merriment. Instead he scans the revellers, hoping by sheer luck to catch sight of Janus again. His eyes linger especially on the dance floor in front of the stage, where he first made her acquaintance so long ago.

He touches his temple in pain, then clutches his stomach where a noisome feeling is whirling and churning. Gathering his gall, George finally pays for his drinks, wiping his beaded brow with a cocktail napkin. Pursing his lips to conceal his nausea, George pushes back from the bar, heading straight for the bathroom.

Coming down the steps from the street-level entrance is none other than Maurice Ravel. George sees Ravel first, and tries edging toward the wall to avoid him. But it's too late, Ravel doffs his flat-brim hat and cuts across the room.

"George…" Ravel says with an inscrutable look.

"Oh… Hello, Maurice," George replies, bracing for more harsh words from his mentor. Neither one has apologised for the row in the rehearsal room.

"I know you're all celebrating," Ravel says. "Didn't mean to crash your little *fête*."

"No worries," George says, willing to bury the hatchet. "Go on and enjoy yourself. I'll be right back – just going to the bathroom. Excuse me."

Ravel follows George into the small hallway leading to the bathroom.

George looks back at Ravel with confusion. "I'll be out in just a second," George says, stepping lightly toward the door, trying not to trigger his unsettled stomach.

Ravel clears his throat with spurious

importance. "It's a shame that the sheep clap their hooves over such trite nonsense."

George stops in his tracks and turns around. He decides it's best to handle Ravel now, rather than let him follow to the toilet stalls, which George wouldn't put past the old fuddy-duddy. When his mentor gets something into his head, it's there until someone unsticks it.

"Well," George says, with a look of mock-politeness. "Ira's never been the strongest writer, but somehow, it *was* well received—"

"Not the lyrics," Ravel says drily. "The *music* was nonsense."

George shudders, as much from the harsh words as from another tremor throughout his stomach lining. "That's a… Well, it's your opinion, I suppose…"

Having thrown George off balance, Ravel closes in, stepping between George and the bathroom door, possessed with a wild look in his eyes. George suffers another rail-spike of nausea, eyelids fluttering.

"I really *want* you to have a chance at greatness," Ravel says. "But you mustn't take any more of these empty-headed theatrical assignments. In fact, tonight would be just the sort of place to bring you out of this funk. Surely there's someone in here who could be your next patron…"

"Stop," George says. "I know you don't mean that…"

"I do, George," Ravel says. "You have talent. I want you to push yourself and go out there and find something… Or someone… To fill that void. Especially if we're going to play together at Carnegie Hall."

George looks back at the stage for a few seconds, eyes instinctively scanning for Janus. Taking a deep breath, he tampers his nausea for another moment. "So, this is just about *your* reputation, then? Because that would explain it…"

Ravel steps back, at last noticing George's sickly pallor. "You don't look so good."

George puts a hand on the door to the bathroom. "You don't say…"

Ravel narrows his eyes, looking annoyed, disappointed and blameful. "Celebration is one thing, George. But if you don't get a hold of yourself, even your precious Broadway crowd is going to notice. And just because I didn't help you dress up your pig of a show in a silken waistcoat, doesn't mean we don't have our work cut out for Carnegie."

Ravel's voice begins to fade in and out. George nods back with affected comprehension. After a final, scrutinising look, Ravel's lips move for the last time, and he leaves George alone in the hallway.

The walls begin shifting and losing clarity. The hallway lights start glowing so brightly that George must clench his eyelids to slits. He sways on his feet and leans into the bathroom door, blindly stumbling inside. Greeted by the smell of the grime-encrusted toilets, a suffocating wave of nausea towers over him. George charges into a stall just in time, filling the porcelain bowl with brown vomit.

When the dry heaving is over, George gets an odd feeling, as if his head were ten times heavier than usual. Tucking his chin down to his chest, his head lolls, drawn down to the floor as if his brain were made of solid marble. George tries to engage his neck muscles, but cannot. He collapses beside the toilet bowl and shuts his eyes, greeted with a surreal, dreamlike vision.

A moulded, marble bust of his brain appears, tumbling on a trickle of water through a drainpipe. The greyish-pink sculpture turns over and over, bringing back gut-wrenching nausea. George opens his eyes, but the bathroom stall is spinning, giving him a feeling much worse than the vision. George curls up around the base of the toilet. Squeezing his eyes shut, he watches his marble-cut brain in the drainpipe. George hears a flushing noise, and the pipe is filled with water, taking George and the sculpture of his brain along with it. His consciousness dimming, George sees a dark green circle at the end of the pipe, finally emerging into dark and murky water.

The bust of his brain tumbles into the deep water. Strangely, his mind doesn't sink. Instead it rises up, and explodes all at once into shards of pale stone. When the fragments are clear, George sees his own body swimming for the surface, as if it had burst out from the shattering cranial mould. George reaches the surface, gasping for air, and swims to the edge of a giant pool. Technicolour fireworks light the sky above. Big-band fanfare plays from somewhere close by.

George crawls over the ledge of the pool, pulling himself out of the water. Shapes come into focus, starting with outdoor furniture sets and umbrellas, then with people attending a crowded party. George looks around in awe at the partygoers. Each of his favourite composers are here, laughing, chatting and sharing hors d'oeuvres. Mozart, Bach, Schubert, and Brahms. Beethoven, Chopin, Handel and Haydn. Then, with his feet hanging off the diving board, he catches sight of Debussy, cocktail in hand.

"Hey," George mumbles, pushing through the crowd.

Mozart laughs rudely. "He can hardly hold himself together."

George is still soaking wet, the tuxedo he rented for opening night ruined. He almost slips and wonders whether he is having some sort of nightmare.

"He's got no form," Bach says to Tchaikovsky.

George heads for the diving board, but Debussy drains his glass and gets up, moving into another throng of classical music legends.

"Hey! Excuse me…" George says, ducking under a waiter's tray of drinks. George circles around a heated tête-à-tête, where Schubert appears to be arguing with Vivaldi. No matter how many of his idols he passes, George knows he must reach Debussy to escape. Stifled by revellers crossing his path, George can barely see Debussy's head bobbing, a smaller and smaller thatch of brown hair, moving endlessly further away.

***

George wakes up the next morning in a cold sweat, without any memory of getting home. Instead of blaming the booze, he allows his increasing addiction to be rationalised. *Must've eaten something gone bad,* he says to himself, then rolls over and fails to get back to sleep. After a few minutes of lying there like a fossil, he gets a surprising boost of energy. Swinging out his legs, he heads to the kitchen, where he drinks a whole pitcher of water to himself.

Ira had slept on the couch that night, because

George had been so sick, someone had to make sure the apartment wasn't repainted in stomach bile. Ira hears George guzzling down the water and stirs out of his own fitful slumber. Yawning, cursing his brother's hazardous habits, Ira pads into the kitchen and sits down.

"Dammit, George," Ira says. "I know we did well last night, but I can't stand guard after every premiere."

"Don't worry," George says. "I feel just fine now! How about some tennis?"

Ira narrows his eyes, but eventually agrees. He knows from his own experience how dreadfully hungover his brother must be, and a tennis court is a better place to vomit than an apartment full of rugs and upholstery. Besides, Ira enjoys catching his brother in a lie.

***

In the Gershwin's old stomping grounds of Brooklyn, New York, a brand-new set of courts has recently been constructed. Ira gets a cab, and the two of them head to Lincoln Terrace Park. Despite his initial confidence, George gets another wave of nausea on the way over, cursing the stop-and-go traffic they run into.

George runs to the bathroom as soon as the cab pulls up, leaving Ira with the fare. Ira is happy to foot the bill, rather enjoying the attempt George is making. Ira knows it's only a matter of time before George is forced to stop pretending he isn't sick. When the fiendish hangover rears its ugly head, Ira plans to have front-row tickets. Otherwise, he won't be able to say, 'I told you so'.

When George comes back from the bathroom, looking pale, Ira play-punches him in the shoulder. "Hey, brother, why the long face?"

"I'm fine," George says grimly. "And by the way, I did *not* just throw up. Just had to go… You saw me drink that pitcher of water."

Ira plays along. "Sure I did! When nature calls…"

George loses the first game narrowly, feeling pretty good, considering the night he had. But when he starts serving in the next game, he double-faults, then double-faults again.

"Hold on," Ira laughs. "Let me get a chair!"

The lines at the far end of the court won't sit still. They keep losing focus and doubling in his vision. "Okay," George says to himself, "this time you got it."

The ball goes up and George makes good contact. But, when he squints to the other side of the court, he sees Ira snickering and checking his fingernails.

"That one was closer," Ira says. "Couple of feet off. Look brother, you wanna get the ball *inside* the box. See this line here?"

"Piss off," George says, taking another ball from his pocket. He bounces it a few times and mutters under his breath, "If the line won't stay still, then screw it, I'm serving blind."

George's next serve finally hits the mark, but Ira smashes it back straightaway. George stumbles on the return. Another point for Ira, who looks over cheerily.

"Hey, George," Ira says. "Don't go and hurt yourself. We can always quit early."

George finally seems to have submitted to the insistent ball and chain of his hangover. His eyes are dark and heavily bagged, not to mention bloodshot and watery. Heaving a sigh, he creaks open a folding chair and sits down. "I can't do the show with Ravel," he mutters.

"What?" Ira shouts. "Couldn't hear from the winning side of the court!"

George wipes his brow with a hand towel, then tosses it in a gesture of defeat.

"Aha!" Ira declares, beaming. "The towel has been thrown!"

George groans and leans back in the flimsy chair, patting his gurgling stomach.

Ira comes over and pulls up a chair beside his ailing brother. "What was it you were saying just now? Something about Ravel?"

George turns his head just enough to make eye contact. His neck muscles are achy and stiff. "I can't do the show at Carnegie Hall."

Ira blinks. "You can't? What are you talking about…? The man came all the way from France! I'm not even complaining that it's scheduled for the last week of Porgy! You *have* to do it, George. Don't be silly."

"Did you see him last night?" George asks.

"No…" Ira says. "He was at the Club?"

George gives a feeble sigh as confirmation.

"Well, did you two get into it again?" Ira asks. "The quarrelling between you two... I swear—"

"It wasn't so bad," George says. "I didn't really take the bait."

"So, what's the problem?" Ira asks.

"I'm afraid I won't measure up," George says.

"Come now," Ira says. "That's the hangover talking. You'll feel better, tomorrow. Don't forget, you're a musical genius, brother. Cut back on the drink, and you'll be just fine. Only thing Ravel has that you don't... is a stick up his ass."

George smiles despite his splitting headache.

"Come on," Ira says, putting a hand on his brother's shoulder. "Let's get home, clean up, and then you can take a nice long nap."

George grins at his brother. "You only won because of my condition, you know."

Ira gets up. "Okay, then. I won't argue... But only if you promise to do the Carnegie show, and get yourself together."

George puts his hand out.

Ira shakes George's hand, then pulls him up out of the chair. "By the way," Ira says. "We're going to Hollywood."

George is struck by an outsized fear. "Hollywood? What?" Overbalanced, he stumbles as Ira lets go of his hand and walks away.

"You knew about this," Ira says, scoffing.

"Knew about Hollywood?" George says tersely, scooping up his racket and following his brother off the court. "Of course, I know where Hollywood is… But not that you'd want to uproot the New York Gershwins all of a sudden! Can't this California dream wait a bit longer?"

Ira spins round at the gate. "Give me one good reason why we shouldn't be gone by the end of the season? Fred's out there… Ginger… even Wally flew the coop! Come on, Hollywood is Broadway, but better. It's summertime year-round!"

"I don't care if we're neighbours with Marion Davies," George says, pouting. "I don't wanna to go to Hollywood."

Ira sighs, giving his brother a condescending look. "It's the money, George. With a single picture, we could make what we make on *three* Broadway shows…"

George stops at the top of stairs, while Ira takes

them two at time, then waves down a cab from the sidewalk.

"Don't run away from me!" George cries. "We're having a conversation!"

A cab pulls up to the kerb, and Ira looks back up the stairs. "You know, brother," he calls, "not everything is always about you!"

George glares at Ira, incensed enough to sock him one, but too light-headed to race down the stairs.

"Getting your own cab, then?" Ira shouts, smirking.

George shakes a fist, but even to himself, the gesture is merely comical, instead of being fearsome like he wanted. Ira ducks into the cab with a wink and a wave, leaving George to find his own way home.

"Well," George mutters. "That one was a blowout. Game, set, match: Ira Gershwin."

***

The following week is spent rehearsing for the upcoming concert at Carnegie Hall. Ravel is set to play opposite Gershwin in a duelling piano format. The stage has been decorated with a line of marble statuettes along the back curtain. There's a bust of Bach, Mozart, Beethoven, and Tchaikovsky. The great composers glare with unblinking eyes out from a fine-sculpted row before the back curtain. Damrosch is up in arms with the tidal wave of complaints coming from Ravel. The French master seems to have lost all semblance of understanding, and forgotten that compromise is universal.

At the afternoon rehearsal, the very last one before the premiere performance, Ravel is embattled in gripes with the lead violinist.

"I will not play on this piano," Ravel cries, making no effort to soften his voice, even in the sepulchral silence of the famous theatre.

The violinist is a clean-shaven man in his late thirties, with a serious demeanour and career musician's pride. He stares at Ravel with incomprehension, wondering why Ravel taking issue with the piano would need to be called to his attention in the first place. Luckily, before the preened professional can start saying something that he might lose his job for, Walter Damrosch appears, cutting in.

Damrosch frowns at Ravel. "Something wrong with the piano... What on earth could it be, Monsieur Ravel?"

"It's completely out of tune," Ravel says with a callow impatience. "The action is potentially damaging to my tendons."

George Gershwin appears, fixing his cufflinks with casual form, his voice breaking in with an almost cynical tone. "It played fine to me," he says to Ravel, simply.

Gershwin's composure may in fact have caused a blood vessel to burst somewhere under Ravel's skin. Despite the simmering pressure in his bloodstream, Ravel diverts his rage over to Damrosch. "It's out of tune, Walter. I cannot play *music* on it. We are here to perform music, no?"

Concealing an exasperated sigh, Damrosch pretends to cough into his handkerchief. "Well then," he says, "I'll send for the tuner."

"Oh no," Ravel hisses. "The tuners you provide are evidently incompetent. For eventualities such as this, I have my own."

"Your own tuners?" Damrosch asks. "In New

York City?"

"Certainly," Ravel sneers. "I cannot take any chances. I will fetch them at once." Ravel lets out a little humph, then spins round on George and Damrosch, who are hastily vacating the stage.

George doesn't see Ravel until much later, when the backstage area is busy with preparations, and the show is set to begin in ten minutes. There's no time for chit-chat, so George can only wonder if Ravel even re-tuned, or if the whole fuss was only an attempt to knock George off balance. Either way, George is nervous and sweat-streaked, having spent the lead up to curtain call in a dissociative state. Not only did Ravel's histrionics induce panic, but George also suffered a worrisome experience, having to do with Debussy's slippers.

The episode had started in the privacy of his dressing room, where George had tried to remove the pungent slippers. Of course he couldn't have worn them during the performance, because Ravel would have noticed. So, after warming up his fingers on the upright piano in his little green room, it was time to remove the slippers. However, much to his surprise, it was rather difficult. Pry and pull as he might, even after asking a stagehand for a shoehorn, the slippers seemed to have grown fond of his feet – they were stuck on.

With the use of the shoehorn and firm grip on the make-up table, George finally yanked off the foul-smelling footwear, at which point his momentum toppled him head-over-heels into a heap on the floor. Wincing, straightening his legs, he caught his breath, but then his stomach began to tumble and turn like an acrobat, and George had to lay flat on the floor to combat the nausea. Not only that, but the shuffle of stagehands and chamber musicians in the hallway grew entirely muffled for almost fifteen minutes. George's vision started to burn away at edges, too, until he was unconscious for at least ten minutes.

Finally, a thudding on the door had awoken him. It was some stagehand with a message from Damrosch. George had shambled to his feet and answered it, receiving the instructions and managing to keep his lunch down. The stagehand had been breathless, with a frightfully folded brow, especially for a man so young. And yet, the stagehand was too preoccupied with his own pre-show duties to even notice Gershwin's sickly state of affairs.

Backstage, these recent memories flash before George's eyes in the last few moments before the show. Damrosch appears to give him a heartening nudge, and George goes to his seat at his grand piano. Meantime, Ravel settles down at the other grand. The two men stare at each other when the curtain rises, revealing an auditorium packed to the gills. Well-dressed ladies peer down from the box seats, elegant gentlemen at their sides.

Gershwin and Ravel both rise from their benches, greeting the crowd with perfunctory bows. The enticement wafting from the audience is emboldening. They're here for *his* new composition, George says to himself. They're here for *him*, and Ravel is a side dish. George is also comforted by the sight of the front row, where Ira, Aimée, Damrosch, Wally, and Kitty are seated and smiling up at him.

All seems on the up and up, until with a heart-stuttering jolt, Ravel sits quickly and begins to play. This is even before the applause has finished, and George must rush to catch up to Ravel's cadence. Thus, begins the duet of *An American in Paris*. Master and student, reunited in the theatre once again.

Frantically trying to keep pace with Ravel, George's hands start to shake on the second movement. His nerves and alcohol dependence are getting to him. George finds himself wishing for a double whisky, going so far as to imagine the amiable, amber liquid, sitting in the stage-light glow on the piano top.

Suddenly – at least to George – the piece reaches a coda. Ravel leaps over an entire half-measure, leaving George lost as to where he should pick up, even though he wrote the music himself. Never a sight-reader, the printed music notes do nothing to guide his way. Ravel plays even faster, with George falling behind by entire strings of notes. Ravel is playing faster than George has ever heard or seen, hammering through the piece like he's tenderising meat.

When another awful headache splits down his cranium, George decides he can't take it anymore. Flourishing with a few discordant notes, he stands up. The piano bench scrapes on the floor as he steps away. Assuming this is part of the act, half the audience starts to clap, then falls into confused, rumbling murmurs. George begins walking off stage, with a final, cursory glance at the front row, where his nearest and dearest look back at him, befuddled.

Nothing left, George disappears into the wings.

Ravel plays on, and the murmuring crowd falls silent again, soon rapt by his blazing performance. A minute or so later, Ravel concludes the piece, rising to a welcoming ovation. Ravel bows, soaking in stolen admiration, strutting from stage left to right, taking extra bows. He gestures to the orchestra and George's empty piano. But George Gershwin is gone from the theatre by now, headed to a bar on some dreary backstreet. Ravel luxuriates in applause for a minute longer, taking a final bow and his exit, while a few ladies in the front row throw roses at his feet.

CHAPTER 15

Several weeks later, Kitty Carlisle walks alone down Park Avenue. Her mascara is streaked, and her eyeshadow is mottled, having just furiously pawed away tears. Sniffling, she clutches a mink to her neck, chilled by an autumn breeze which bargains for winter. Kitty deftly navigates the sidewalk cracks, pinpoint high heels clicking her along. Seeing a phonebooth, she makes her way towards it. The outside is scuffed and layered with profanities in permanent marker. Inside the booth, it's clean and very warm.

Kitty dials a number from memory. *Trill... Trill...* says the phone, but nobody picks up. By now, Kitty's eyes are welling with more tears. Finally, she hangs up and chokes back a sob, looking back to make sure a queue hasn't formed. Then, with a shuddering breath, she wipes her eyes, fishing a card case out from her purse. Flipping through contact cards at a gallop, she lets the unused ones scatter the floor, akin to the maples and oaks along the avenue, which are losing their first leaves of the season.

Somebody picks up this time. A man's voice.

"Where is he, Ira?" Kitty asks. "I must see him. I've been going out of my mind with worry."

Ira's voice is tinny and muffled. "There's nothing to worry about. He's in perfectly good hands."

"Can I visit him?" Kitty asks, breathless again. "Can you just give me the name of the hospital?"

There's a moment of silence on the other line. Anxiety spreads through the booth like a deadly gas.

Before Kitty can ask him again, Ira answers. "I'm not sure that's such a good idea. He doesn't want to be disturbed."

"Don't do this," Kitty pleads. "I'm begging you, Ira—"

"Kitty…" Ira sighs. "There's no cause for concern. Doc says he's gonna be well enough to fly. He told you about Hollywood, right?"

"Hollywood?" Kitty asks, even more flustered. "What are you talking about?"

Another long and dreadful silence follows.

Finally, Ira says, "Dammit George... Okay, Kitty. It's like this— We've got a contract to score a motion picture. The money's too good to stay in New York. Leonore just got in... I can't talk much longer, okay? Point is... don't worry. I'm sure he's gonna write you." Ira's voice wavers. He doesn't sound sure at all.

"Ira, no," Kitty cries. "I've gotta speak to him, please!"

Ira's voice fades. He's talking to someone else, covering the receiver.

"I gotta go," Ira says. "Take care of yourself, and I'll have him call you."

"Ira! Wait, Ira, please..." Kitty sobs, breaking down completely as Ira hangs up.

Kitty drops the phone and slumps the floor. Clouds gather overhead, threatening rain. Kitty cries until the glass panels are misted over, and the operator comes onto the line.

"Hello?" the operator says. "I'm sorry, but I have to disconnect this call..."

Kitty shakes from another wave of unbridled tears. The phone line goes dead, leaving a buzzing drone. The only remaining sounds are Kitty's choking sobs, and the wind wailing the vitreous, cold shell of the phonebooth.

***

Los Angeles weather is good for George Gershwin. After his hospital-scare in New York, he's soon back to his heavily intoxicated self, working away on the movie score with Ira. Months pass by in a haze. The sunshine is just like Ira said it would be. Eternal, undaunting, unrelenting. Under its warm rays, George gathers his strength, and finds himself even more inclined to his old vices. Hollywood George is driven simply by pleasure, which he not only derives from composing and playing music, but the classic old vices of booze and women. Both of which are presented in teeming supply.

A typical tableau – January sun, barely diminished. A thin, marine-layer cover of clouds. Ocean breeze at a poolside celebrity affair. A swarthy and lush George Gershwin playing piano, having switched his trousers for white linen shorts.

Ira Gershwin, making his rounds with a tray of cocktails, beaming and laughing with all the other stars. He serves one each to Ginger Rogers and Paulette Goddard, who then make their way over to George, sitting prettily down on either side of him.

Paulette touches his knee. Ginger leaves in a dainty little huff.

Paulette feigns embarrassment. "Do you think I've upset her?"

"No, no. Blame it on me," George slurs. "You're perfect."

"No Georgie…" Paulette coos in his ear. "You are."

George takes another sip of his drink with a shaky grip. A wet ring leaves a mark on the wooden piano lid. Paulette slides closer to George on the bench. "You do realise Charles is in Paris this weekend?"

"Oh really?" George asks, gurgling his whisky. "I've been there, you know… Nice city."

"Yes," Paulette sighs, batting her eyes. "Leaving me here alone in our big empty house. All because they wanna give him some award. Well, you want to know what I think?"

"Sure, baby…" George says, fiddling with the piano keys.

Paulette flips her flowing black hair over her shoulder. "I think the French are the only people who think he's funny these days."

George laughs heartily, which turns into coughing to clear the ice from his throat.

Paulette pats him on the back, taking the chance to sidle up even closer. "You okay? Need some water?"

"No, no," he waves her off. "Your husband, Charlie… Well, I'm an American, and I still think he's funny… A funny little man… Wait – can you smell burning rubber?"

George falls flat on the piano keys. Paulette's heart takes a leap into her throat, and the whole party turns to the crashing, discordant noise. Ira comes over and tends to his brother, both Gershwins leaving in a hurry. Embarrassed beyond belief, Ira needs help dragging his unconscious brother to the car. All the while, Ira tries to bandage his reputation with a string of hastily crafted, apologetic farewells, not only to the hosts, but to all the guests he was hoping to impress.

***

That evening at the Santa Monica beach house, Leonore sits by the open window, listening to the surf. Ira has just put George into bed. Coming into the living room, Ira watches his wife for a moment, loving her even more now in this crisis. Ira is overwhelmed with concern for his brother, but filled with love for dependable Leonore. He walks over to where she's perched on the window seat, then sits behind her and cradles her in his arms.

Leonore looks up, face full of worry. "Will you believe me now? The same thing happened last week."

"He's just tired. He came out here to relax and he's relaxed too much."

"That's not relaxing. He's ill. I can't... I won't have him here. He needs help, Ira, he needs to be somewhere else..."

"He drinks a little too much, I grant you..."

"He can't even hold his fork at the dinner table. It's an embarrassment."

"What are you saying? You don't want my brother living here?"

But Leonore is already convinced. "He's sick. I'm sorry Ira, but I can't have him here until he promises to get clean."

They discuss what to do in hushed voices. Even though Ira made sure George had gone to sleep, the walls are thin, and they don't want to wake him. Leonore's voice is even lower than Ira's. She doesn't trust George not to start thrashing in his typical spate of night terrors, waking himself up in shivers and shakes. Or else, she tells Ira, George might've pretended to fall asleep, and could even be eavesdropping on their plans.

Ira tells his wife that she's being paranoid, but Leonore keeps to a whisper all the same. Firm and self-assured, she makes it as clear as a Louis Armstrong high note. "Brother or not... there's something really wrong with him. This is our home, and he can't stay here anymore until I hear it from him that he wants to change."

The argument goes on until both of their cigarette packages are empty. Too tired to run for more smokes, Ira and Leonore decide to figure something out in the morning, heading off to bed where they both sleep deeply.

Just before midnight, the telephone rings. Leonore bolts upright, heartbeat thudding. She leans over Ira and tries to shake him awake. Ira groans a murmur in his sleep, so Leonore waits for the line to stop ringing. But it doesn't. Finally, she goes to the hallway and answers.

"Hello? Yes... He's here with us, but he's sleeping. Speaking of which, might I ask why you're calling so late? Oh... jet lag... I see... Okay... Well I think George would love to discuss that... You're here in LA? Hmm... All right... Leaving soon? I see... Perhaps he can meet you in the next few days. I'll put your name down and tell him you called... That's Janus? Uh-huh... J-A-N..."

***

Leonore was right. George had been faking sleep. Having snuck out when Ira and Leonore had gone to bed, now he pushes his roadster down the drive in neutral. When he reaches the street, he starts up the engine and stops off at a liquor store in Hollywood. Half an hour later, the fifth of Tennessee whisky is half-guzzled. George drives along the perilous curves of Laurel Canyon.

The lights of Los Angeles look like a second set of stars, underneath the real ones in the dark, sheltering sky. George hums to himself, shutting his eyes with pleasure, then nearly collides with an oncoming car. He swerves and almost over-corrects, but after a squealing of tyres and flashing of red brake lights, George gets the vehicle straightened out. Even so, his eyes are glossy beyond recognition. The bottle of whisky lies on the passenger seat. George's eyes wander to the view out the window, where city lights begin to sparkle and pop, turning into what looks like a firework show to George.

Two hours later, George finally pulls back up to the beach house. This time, he doesn't bother to turn off the engine and push the car in neutral. Instead, he screeches to halt, stumbling out without even cutting the headlights. He wobbles inside to the front room, where Ira and Leonore are both waiting up for him.

"George," Ira shouts. "Where in God's name

have you been?"

"Nowhere and everywhere," George slurs in a sing-song manner. "Don' worry, brother. I'm fine, just fine…"

Leonore sighs. "I told you so."

Ira is about to admonish his brother, but with a look at Leonore, they decide they're both too tired for any sort of emotion other than relief. George is safe again, and that's what matters.

"You were right," Ira says to his wife. "I'll take him to bed."

Leonore squeezes his hand, then heads upstairs.

Ira gets to his brother just in time, as George has just very nearly knocked down a flowerpot. Ira drapes an arm around George, then leads him off to his bedroom.

"Get your mind right, buddy," he whispers with a mixture of love and vexation. "We've got pictures to score. Big money to make, awards with our name on 'em. We're gonna be remembered forever."

Upon reaching the bedroom, George's body slumps forward onto the bed. Ira throws an extra quilt over him, and tugs off George's shoes. Pausing at the doorway to turn off the light, Ira doesn't notice the lifeless look on George's darkened face. Ira walks away to deal with the car, leaving Leonore alone to see George's eyes roll back in his head.

CHAPTER 16

Less than a year later, George Gershwin's mental condition is beyond repair. The night of George's failed brain surgery and subsequent death, Dr Dandy sits in the temporary office the hospital has provided. The door creaks open slowly, but he fails to notice.

Dandy is smoking a pipe, filling the room with smoke, while he writes up his report for the surgery; the operation which was already a lost cause when he arrived. While Dandy is signing on the very last line, a dark shadow falls over him. He looks up without so much as capping his pen, meeting eyes with Maurice Ravel, who stands in the open doorway like an angel of death.

"May I help you?" Dandy asks. "It's long past normal hours."

"Is he gone yet?" Ravel asks.

Dandy wrinkles his brow. "I'm sorry?"

"The legendary pianist," Ravel clarifies. "Is he

dead?"

"Gershwin?" Dandy asks, surprised at how fast the news has travelled.

Ravel steps forward and looms over Dandy. "That's the one."

"Unfortunately, Sir, I'm in no position to…" Suddenly, Dandy recognises the shadow face above him. "Ah!" Dandy cries, impressed by his own memory. "You're that chap that learned from Debussy! Something with an 'R'. Ravine… No, Ravel!"

"Right," Ravel says. "If he's gone, then, I take it he didn't mention me?"

"What?" Dandy asks.

Ravel sits down on the side of the desk. "You were his surgeon. You were there when he… Never mind. Look, it's a simple question – did he mention me?"

Dandy frowns. "I'm sorry, Sir. Not that I know of."

"What were his last words?" Ravel asks, suffering a jealous shiver.

"I don't know," Dandy says. "He was unconscious when I got there."

"For Heaven's sake," Ravel says impatiently. "What did he say? Anything? What were his regrets? Did he say he stole the slippers?"

"Sir," Dr Dandy says coolly. "I don't have the slightest idea. I'm sorry."

Ravel looks wistfully away, into the light of the empty hallway. "If people on their deathbeds don't make an utterance... is it because they never found the right words, or never had anything to say in the first place?"

Dandy sighs, getting up and arranging his paperwork. "To be candid, Mr Ravel – he was dead when I arrived... The man had severe mental anguish and problems with his mental faculties. Judging by the state he was in, I'm not sure his last words would've had much weight."

A moment passes before Ravel speaks. "Well, his prominence was fleeting. That may have been a burden on the mind. A man without the power of will for last words, I can only assume he'll be forgotten." Ravel chuckles grimly. "Take it from an artist who shouldn't have outlived him."

Dandy crosses the room and heads for the door. "I wouldn't be so sure. Those who die young...

Those are the ones we remember."

Ravel turns ghastly pale. "And those of us who live full lives?"

Dr Dandy lingers politely in the doorway, although he's clearly ready to end the conversation. "It depends," the doctor says. "But you live in Paris, no?"

Ravel nods, unsure why he's being asked.

"Then in Gershwin's case," Dr Dandy says, "you just crossed over an ocean for a dead man. Maybe that's the mark of a real, legacy."

Ravel turns the words over in his head, wondering if the doctor is wise, or just lucky with an uncertain guess. Either way, Ravel tilts his chin in his typical way, looking down his nose with a minuscule nod, serving as a silent farewell. Then, the French master whips up his overcoat and sweeps into the hallway, squeaking his heels on the shiny, buffed floors.

Watching Maurice Ravel traipse away, a look of amusement appears on Dandy's face. When the Frenchman reaches the end of the hallway, he dips around the corner and out of sight. Dandy shrugs, gathering his briefcase and overcoat, then leaves the office where he meets with his military escort again. The officers arrange for a car to his hotel, where Dandy goes straight to the bar for a stiff drink.

***

Four and a half months later, it's early evening in the sitting room of the Ravel chateau. Maurice is propped in a wheelchair, with a quilt over his legs. His face is pallid and drawn. Moisture collects under his nose and around his lips. He's suffering from Pick's disease, declining steadily in the past few months, his brain beset by the chronic disorder.

Aimée sits across the room, reading by lamplight.

"Did I do that to him?" Ravel asks.

Aimée looks up. "What?"

"Did I do that to him?" Ravel asks once more. "Gershwin, I mean…"

"Would you like some water?" Aimée asks, ignoring his question.

Ravel's mind is just barely strong enough to

know that he's been ignored. He gives Aimée a dirty look, then winces from a sudden jolt of pain, "I need to see George's grave…"

"Oh… Maurice," Aimée sighs. "Maybe not now. Let's get you a little more rest…"

"I want to see the headstone…" Ravel croaks weakly.

Aimée attempts to smile, but feeling a rush of sudden despair, she steps away from the bed instead, drying her eyes on a frilled sleeve. She goes to a tall cabinet and produces a travelling case. It's peeling, tattered, and imbued with strange energy. It makes her think of the phone call from Ira Gershwin, about a month after George's death, and the arrangements made to return the decaying slippers to the chateau. Stifling tears, she returns the bedside.

"I'll tell you what," Aimée says. "If you can put these on, and walk over to the desk and back, then we can discuss it all in the morning."

She sets the box in his lap. Ravel summons all his strength, reaching for the handle. Aimée supports his elbow to help him open it, but Ravel pushes her hand away with a gasp. The box falls to the floor, but doesn't open.

Aimée retrieves it and puts her hands on the clasps. "You want to have a look, huh?"

Ravel nods in resignation.

Aimée opens the travelling trunk and sets it in his lap. "Shall we go by the fire?"

Ravel nods again, and she wheels him close to the fire, then goes back to her chair.

Ravel looks down at the slippers in the trunk, a single, silent tear running down his face. The fire is warm, and he wiggles his toes beneath the blanket. He starts to hear Gershwin's music in his head, but soon enough his eyelids begin to droop. He's a very tired man.

"Aimée," he murmurs. "I'm off to bed."

Aimée looks up from her book, confused. But Ravel throws the quilt off his legs, then pushes his feet into Debussy's slippers. Aimée stays quiet, unable to believe what she's seeing. Ravel grabs the cane on the side of the wheelchair. It slides from the carrying sleeve without a sound, even though it hasn't come loose in months. Ravel stands up with his weight on the cane, then limps slowly out of the sitting room. Aimée watches his shadow shrinking in the amber firelight.

When she goes to check on him later, he's tucked himself into bed and appears to be sound asleep. She sets a glass of water on his bedside table, then checks to see that his chest is still rising and falling. Aimée leans in to kiss Ravel's cheek, then goes to the door where she pauses on the threshold. Shaking her head, she murmurs to herself, "Still… after all these years, you amaze me."

Aimée shuts the door with a soft click. Half a moment later, Ravel dives into a deep darkness, from which he does not emerge for a very long time.

CHAPTER 17

Aimée, Marianne, and Madame Du Vollé handle the funeral and proceedings. Beyond the veil, it's as if a single candle is lit with each earthly day. A white light grows ever brighter, until Ravel's spirit begins to stir in its slumber. At last, one fine temporal day, Ravel's bare essence returns to awareness, graced by the sight of a bright, liminal space.

Blinking, Ravel raises a stunningly weightless hand, shielding his transparent face from the light. Sheer and blinding though it is, the light is rather warm, and softens as Ravel's eyes start to adjust, bringing into focus the geometric planes of an untrammelled reality. Once he remembers how to walk, Ravel strides up to a bow-shaped reception desk, moulded out of gleaming white marble.

A young female clerk is perched at the desk, which has a fine halo of mist all around it. The young woman's face is pink as a cherub. She smiles impassively at Ravel. Behind her are great puffy plumes of foggy clouds, covering a far-off range of steep mountains, each of which is capped with a snow-stricken peak. The young woman beams down at him, glowing with purity. She seems to be patiently waiting…

Waiting…

Waiting for Ravel to remember who she is.

"Excuse me," Ravel says, winding up to his full height. Puffing up his chest, his pomp and self-righteous demeanour come flooding back. Before he knows it, the words have rolled off his tongue. "I am Maurice Ravel."

The woman's face changes ever so slightly. A little grandiose, but his affirmation seems to have stamped his ticket. Ravel clears his throat, trying to appear modest.

"Good," the young woman says. Her voice is a crystal carillon. "Mr Ravel, I'll be taking you through security. Just a few questions. Chamber or orchestral?"

"Orchestral," Ravel replies.

"Home key signature?" she asks.

"G major," he answers.

"And... your mother's maiden name?" the young woman asks.

"Delouart," Ravel says. "You know, I've had this dream before—"

The clerk snaps her fingers. "That's it! Well done, you just crossed over."

"I'm sorry?" Ravel asks.

"I would be too," she says. "Finally, what is the first and last letter of your most regrettable, yet most *popular* work?"

"Oh, er..." Ravel turns as pink as her cherubic cheeks. "That's 'B' and 'O'."

"Thank you," the woman says, her voice still clear as a crystalline bell. "Welcome to *Reputation Heaven*. Year of death: 1937. You'll be shacked up in the conservative/modernist suite. Here's your key card!"

Ravel takes the mag-card reader from her powder-white hand, feeling it pulling him, leading him along. Before he can say goodbye, the key card yanks him away. Ravel is soon flying through misty, billowing clouds, rocketing through pockets of freezing, condensed air. Ravel shuts his eyes to keep them from watering, and the last thing he wants is to let go of the key card, even though it's the very thing propelling him forward. He'd rather be headed somewhere than lost in the pale mist.

Next moment, Ravel tumbles out on a flat surface. The floor here is velvet-smooth, and his legs find purchase quickly, the key card pulling him up to his feet, where he trots up to a high, stainless-steel door. Ravel has never seen anything quite so modern-looking. The key card draws his hand toward a gunmetal grey box, whereupon Ravel grips the card as it swipes through the slot. A green light glows on a card-reader box, triggering a few notes of 'Bolero' from inside. The massive steel door begins to shake. Not a moment later, the door is sliding upward, slowly and silently, releasing a cloud of warm steam through the door jamb, shrouding Ravel in a sense of belonging.

Ravel steps forward, vision all steamy and totally occluded. Stepping through the door frame, another scene begins to find its form, this one in brand-new colours and odd, mysterious shapes. Each novel object triggers an old memory. A pink, inflatable, donut for example: a *pool toy*. The pool toy has a person inside, laid-back and drifting. Holding a cocktail in his hand. There's a pool of liquid around the floating man, and more and more people sharpen into view. By this sort of memory-induction and association, the scenario before him sketches its own solidity.

There's a bright-blue swimming pool shaped like a kidney bean, at the helm of which is a soundstage with a DJ, who's busy playing the all-time 'classical music hits'. Spotting Ravel, the DJ takes up a wireless mic and starts bellowing. "Hey now, lookee here, Maurice Ravel made it in! Let's give him a big ol' *Reputation Heaven* welcome!"

A scattered applause trickles in from the crowd, all of whom are dressed in clean, white suits with black bow ties. Ravel smiles meekly and gives a small wave to his fellow partygoers. The DJ mixes the Bach concerto back in, while everyone at the poolside returns to their conversation. The heavy steel door has disappeared behind him, so Ravel has no choice but to walk into the melee.

Luckily, he catches sight of the bar, just off to the left of the sound stage. Ravel walks timidly toward it, vaguely knowing somehow that such a place is known for its creature comforts. The bar is being patronised by all the big names of Western Art music – both young and old. Ravel gets excited when he starts to recognise the people on the barstools, but before he makes it there, something hard and wet hits him smack in the face. Sputtering, he spins round and sees a ball rolling away. He stumbles to pick it up, nearly dropping it and calling more ridicule to himself.

Lenny Bernstein waves his hand from the pool "Over here, Maurice!"

In the deep end of the swimming pool, Bernstein is playing water polo with Mozart, Strauss and Schoenberg.

"Watch where you're smashing that thing!" Ravel calls, tossing the ball to Bernstein.

"Thanks, Maurice!" Bernstein calls out, then turns to the right and yells even louder, "Hey, George!"

Ravel pricks up his ears. *George*. But it couldn't be Gershwin, could it?

In fact, it is, and Ravel catches sight of the Brooklynite composer, swarthy, sipping a tumbler of dark liquor, laid up on a sunbed with an ashtray at his side.

"Get in here and help me out," Bernstein hollers. "New York Yankees versus the Viennese Vanguard!"

George switches his drink for a cigar, takes a long puff, then blows a clever smoke ring. "Sorry, Lenny, maybe next game!"

Ravel goes over to George on the sunbed. "Gershwin?" Ravel asks, voice unsteady with outright surprise.

"Oh," George gushes. "How do ya' do, Maurice?"

"I was just telling Aimée..." Ravel stammers, still a bit shocked. "How I wanted to see your grave—"

"Well I guess you never made it," George says impassively, puffing his cigar.

This last burden of guilt blown away in a cloud of smoke, Ravel finally loosens up, buying into the idea that he's really in Heaven after all. "Never made it," Ravel says. "So, what kind of a place lets a charlatan like you in?"

George laughs, setting down his cigar and grabbing his drink again. "I didn't have a choice! I'm in. And... guess who else is?"

Ravel follows the direction of Gershwin's gaze, spotting Claude Debussy at the edge of the pool. Seized with energy, he bustles over to Debussy, abandoning Gershwin.

"Hey," George calls in mock dismay, "what gives?"

"Claude! Claude!" Ravel begins yelping, weaving between groups of composers.

Hearing his name, Debussy turns around. "Oh... You."

"Ah... There are so many things you missed," Ravel blubbers, misty-eyed. "I had a good life, I promise!"

"Didn't miss a wink. I've seen it all, and thank goodness I went when I did. Any more success on my part, and you would've been driven mad decades before."

"Well, I..." Ravel is confused by this cryptic response. "I did what I could to keep your legacy alive!"

"Ah... Ravel, tais-toi. You can be so pompous! The legacy of France... Mon Dieú! Those ridiculous, stinking slippers that you held in such regard." Debussy sighs with a pitying look. "Those nasty slippers were a gift from my mother in law. I hated the tawdry things on sight!"

"But, but…" Ravel is severely shaken. "Then why did you give them to me?"

"Because…" Debussy pauses for a moment, as if considering how to explain gravity to a baby. "I gave you the slippers because I didn't like you. Snapping at my heels! So, I spun you a yarn about lineage and inheritance, a story which you swallowed utterly whole."

Debussy finishes his drink – a Kir cocktail – then turns on his heel, tossing Ravel an apathetic wave. "There you have it, Maurice! À toute à l'heure!"

Ravel's mouth hangs open, but not a word comes out. George walks up and lays a friendly paw on his shoulder. "So… How'd that go?"

Ravel pivots on George, enraged. "You expect me to forget that you leeched off me! You stole the slippers, then made all those scrabbly jazz creations! Sickening!"

"Wait a minute," George chuckles. "I leeched?"

"You know what I'm talking about," Ravel hisses, then looks around at the pool party. "This man, George *Gershwin*. This man is a thief!"

The other composers climb out of the pool, begin moving closer in from the edges of the party, and all gather around, smelling a fight. The DJ turns the volume quite low, bringing the whole pool deck into earshot.

"The slippers again?" George asks, incredulous. "You got them back when I died. And Debussy just told you there was nothing special about them! If anything, they made us crazy because they *didn't* work! Well, I did you a favour by having them. You're the one who lived longer, you should be apologising to me! But you don't see *me* crying out for an apology…"

Ravel glares at Gershwin. "If you were a decent human being, you wouldn't have stolen them. And just because they made you an alcoholic with a rotten brain, doesn't mean they did the same to me! Oh…" Ravel groans, "just think of the pieces I would've written. The slippers belonged to me, and to the country of France!"

"Give it up, Maurice!" George shouts, getting into Ravel's face.

The crowd begins to murmur, cheering on the scuffle.

Ravel bumps George with his forehead. "That's Maurice *Ravel* to you!"

As the men bicker and taunt each other drily, a ring of composers starts to form around them. George points around at their famous faces. "Okay, *Ravel*. That's Wolfgang *Mozart*. And that's Johann *Bach*... And that's Pyotr *Tchaikovsky*. And that's..." George points in every direction he can. "That's *who*ever and this is *what*ever sort of Heaven we want! We're dead! Don't you understand? None of it matters now!"

Following that comment, the air becomes chilly. George tries to put his hand on Ravel's shoulder, but Ravel shrugs it off.

"Okay, Ravel... I admired you." George shrugs. "You set a standard for me to live up to, and I always thought I had your blessing."

Ravel sighs, as if that was all he needed to hear. "Well you didn't, and I should have given it to you. I was petty... but you didn't need my blessing to become great. Listen..."

Debussy steps into the circle, crooning to the tune of his 'Clair De Lune'. "Don't be sore that some hated you," he sings to Ravel. "You can be sure they underrated you… I'm sure that they'll all agree… note for note… you were far better than me…"

Debussy takes a deep breath and turns to Gershwin. "Don't be ashamed that you sold some songs… The world loves dancing and sing-a-longs. You may be too flash and lacking real depth… but that didn't stop you…"

"From slipper theft!" Ravel cries. George rolls his eyes.

"We all steal, Maurice," Debussy sings on. "We all plunder… We're all as guilty and as blameless as each other… What does it matter here as long as we've all been heard? Even John Cage is here, and he hasn't said a word…"

The other composers join in, and soon enough their voices are all swelling to a chorus. "It doesn't matter if you're Impressionist or Expressionist…"

Stravinsky chimes in, "Neo-classicist!"

John Adams bellows, "Postmodernist, minimalist or cubist!"

"Or Exhibitionist!" George sings in a reedy voice.

"Sheer perfectionist!" Ravel drones haughtily.

Tchaikovsky jumps in, "Sad, pathetic, Late-Romanticist!"

"Dangerously populist…" Wagner sings, lilting. "Square-headed, proto-fascist or fugueist…"

"Even Brahms and Liszt…" Debussy wails. "You've got the gist of it… We made some noise… and we're the best at it!"

The composers take rank in a tap-dancing ensemble, replica slippers appearing on their feet. A flamboyant group wades into the shallow end, joining up in a synchronised swim routine, pirouetting around an inflatable floating slipper. Gershwin and Ravel make nice with each other, taking up a Fred and Ginger two-step, whirling round and dipping each other on the arm, and at last falling back into the troupe.

THE END

Printed in Great Britain
by Amazon

58092590R00188